grl2grl

grl2grl

short fictions by JULIE ANNE PETERS

Megan Tingley Books
LITTLE, BROWN AND COMPANY
New York ✢ Boston

Also by Julie Anne Peters:

Define "Normal"
Keeping You a Secret
Luna
Far from Xanadu
Between Mom and Jo

Little, Brown and Company

Hachette Book Group USA
237 Park Avenue, New York, NY 10017
Visit our Web site at www.lb-teens.com

First Edition: September 2007

ISBN-13: 978-0-316-01343-7 (pb)
ISBN-10: 0-316-01343-9 (pb)

10 9 8 7 6 5 4 3 2 1

Q-MT

Printed in the United States of America

To all the young readers who've shared their stories with me

grl2grl

SHORT FICTIONS

Passengers

She sits alone. In Art, senior seminar, lunch, on the train. She always sits alone. If I was alone I'd find something to do. Read or work on homework or doodle, fake it, so if I *was* alone it'd look like I wanted to be alone.

Not her. She sits — slumps — in her seat on the train and stares out the window, down the aisle. She watches me getting on.

I don't look away. Every day we have this stare down. Ten, twenty seconds. We never talk or say hello. Never, How's it going? What's up? I'm not sure she even knows my name.

I sit with my group, always. Becca says, "Did you hear what happened at Ozzy's party?"

I have to force myself to listen. Or care. I have to concentrate hard on not looking at *her*.

"Ozzy and Laura hooked up."

People talk about her. Guys mostly. They call her a dyke. Girls call her a guy. She isn't a guy. Or a girl, really. She's "questionable." Gender fluid.

She's not committing one way or the other, let's just say. Who says you have to? Why do we have to? If I want to dress like a guy, so what? I don't, but if I did . . .

"They're together now."

She wears shapeless clothes — long-sleeved men's shirts and baggy pants. A loose vest over the shirt occasionally. Scuffed leather shoes, like Martens, but not label. She'd never wear labels. She defies labels.

I wonder what she's covering. Or covering up.

My eyes are glued to the back of her head.

She used to have shaggy short hair that looked like someone had taken dull scissors to and hacked off in a rage. This year she'd come back from summer vacation with orangey platinum streaks, clumps all over her head. Angry, but colorful.

The tiny hoop in her left earlobe and three studs up the rim of her ear are the most feminine things about her. Besides her lips. Her lips are wide, puffy, unnaturally large, overly ripe lips. And — get this — she wears red lipstick.

Not cherry red or ruby red. More like brutal, nasty red. Not glossy. Matte. Guys make smooching sounds behind her back. Girls go, *Slut*.

She's not a slut, or jock, or stoner. People don't know what to label her. You have to be a token, you know, to have a seat on the train.

On a whim, I get up and slide into the seat across and behind her. Becca calls, "Tam," and I wave her off, like maybe I want to sit alone for once? Better view. The lips. God, they're huge. Like a slow-mo close-up, they part and her tongue extends and circles the outlined oval of her mouth, moistening every millimeter of lip skin. Her head slowly turns and her eyes raise to meet mine. She fixes on me, suggesting something lewd with her tongue.

I jerk and — CRASH! — the stack of books on my lap falls to the floor, jolting everyone on the train awake. She looks back over her shoulder, to my group, impassive.

∞

"Where are you going?" Becca asks when I stand up at lunch and lift my tray.

I don't answer. It's crazy. I don't know why I'm doing this. The sight of her sitting alone at the picnic table on the cafeteria patio when it's below zero out. What's that about? No one would think to eat outside today; no one's even gone out to smoke at the wall.

A suction, a force, a magnetic pull draws me to the outside door. She startles a little when I slide in the bench across from her. "Anyone sitting here?" I ask.

She blinks. Doesn't say anything for a long minute. Then, "Yeah. I'm saving it for Mr. Right."

That makes me laugh — almost.

She pushes up to leave and I lunge across the table to grab her arm. "I just want to talk to you."

Her gaze hovers over my hand. It rises slowly to my face. Stare down. I'm not letting go. I've gotten this far. She shifts her eyes over my head. Hold, hold. What's there? The wall. A dead tree.

Freezing is the operative word here. "Could we go inside?" I ask. "It's like fifty below. Your lips are blue."

It's meant to be a joke, but I'm the only one laughing — inside.

Her head swivels to take in the crowded cafeteria.

"I know a place," I say, "where we can be alone."

That gets her attention. I didn't mean it like that. Did I? She eyes me again, up and down. Slowly, with that mocking sensuality, she smiles. I release her arm and hug myself in my thin hoodie. If I'd known I was trekking to the Yukon today, I'd have worn mukluks.

"Why?"

"What?"

She's smiling at me. Like her face is stuck. Her eyes are surgical probes.

Why? It's a good question. Why now? The train wreck. That's why now. The train wreck in India. I saw it on the news. This passenger train derailed on a bridge and went plunging into the Krishna River. They didn't have the actual footage of the event, only the aftermath. The wreckage.

A train wreck in India has nothing to do with me, but I started having nightmares afterward. I'd see the people on the train riding along all nonchalant, reading their papers or rocking their babies, trusting they were going to be alive an hour later. Then BAM! The moment of disaster. As people realize what's happening, their mouths gape open in a silent scream.

It jolts me awake and my heart pounds. A long time has to pass, lying awake in the dark, for that vision to dissipate. In that blitz of time, the interminable instant before certain death, do people reach out for each other? Do they embrace or hold hands or hang on to each other? Or do they die alone, not knowing the person sitting next to them? Not even knowing their name. I mean, they're going to be spending eternity together. They should say hello.

Always in the vision she's there. We're falling.

Our train clatters over the Carbondale Bridge every day.

I meet her eyes and say, "I just want to talk to you. Is that so random?" I don't say, I want to know you. Who you are. I don't say, I want to get behind your facade, throw back your cover and reveal you. I want to see your lips move, watch them part, understand how they connect to the rest of your person. I want you to know my name.

Between a slight gap in her lips, I see her teeth chatter. Most of all I want to understand this power you have over me, I think. This . . . surge. Her inner lips are a bruising shade of purple. Mine must be too. We're both shivering.

"Come on. You made your point."

"Which is?" she asks.

Okay, that's it. This isn't worth it. This is so not worth it. Stupid train in India, half a world away. My senior year, with time running out. Forget it, I think. There's no connection. Freeze if you want. I get up and slide out of the bench.

"Just a minute."

My charge for the door slows.

She breaks up the rest of her sandwich and tosses it toward the wall. Four or five sparrows flitter down off the tree, hop over, chitter, vie for choice pickings. Retrieving her backpack from beside her on the bench, she stands and says, "I'm ready."

Oh, *she's* ready. I'm derailed and she's ready.

I feel a sense of relief, though. A shiver of . . . excitement.

∞

I only know about the boneyard because the librarian asked a bunch of us to help her cart a set of encyclopedias in there from the media center during spring cleanup last year. She called it the Britannica Boneyard.

"It's unlocked," I say, turning the knob and pushing in the door with my shoulder. What was I going to do if it was locked? I hadn't thought that far ahead. I enter and hold the door open for her. "I hope there's heat in here."

She passes me. She takes her time, her shoulder brushing mine. There's heat all right. Her eyes dart around all the bookcases and cardboard boxes and shelves of construction paper and art supplies, the old lost-and-found bins, the leftover banners and buttons from ancient pep rallies. I let the door go and it slams shut.

She whirls and crouches like a cat.

"I'm not going to attack you," I say. "God."

A grin tugs at her lips. "Who says I won't attack *you*?"

I exaggerate a sneer. But my stomach jumps.

She drops her backpack with a thud, not scaring me. She doesn't scare me. What scares me is this feeling that there's something enormous here. Explosive. Behind this door, this wall.

Okay. I take a deep breath. After all these years, I'm finally doing it. She's always been different, a loner. Even in middle school. She's ridden my same train since seventh grade. We've exchanged zero words in five years.

That's just wrong.

I've been aware of her on the periphery. Circling in, closer and closer. Who's been circling? Her, or me?

She jams her clunky shoe onto a cardboard box to, like, test the lid. It's solid, full of books or something. She plops down and slumps over. Her spine has a natural curve. Like

Rodin's Thinker. Like an arch bridge. There's a rolling step stool and I pull it over in front of her to sit.

"I'm Tamlyn, by the way," I inform her. "Tam."

She raises her eyes and gives me a look.

"What? I didn't know if you knew that."

Silence.

I go on, "This is where you say, 'I'm Andrea.'"

She betrays her surprise with a blink.

"Or whatever you want to be called."

Her eyes drop and she points to my feet. "What are those?"

"What?"

"Those shoes. What do you call them? Are they comfortable?" she asks.

I elevate my right foot an inch off the floor. My platform geriatrics catch a flicker of fluorescent light and the buckle shines. "Not really. It's what everyone's wearing. Excellent flotation devices in the event of a water landing."

She doesn't laugh. She never laughs. I wonder what her laugh sounds like.

"You want to try them on?"

She reels back like I've threatened to infect her with AIDS. "The gangrenous toe rot hasn't flared up in months," I tell her.

Is that a smile? Did I amuse her?

My insides are a snarl of worms.

I unbuckle my left shoe and pass it to her. She takes a whiff. Please. I give her the right shoe. She regards them for an extended period of time before reaching down to slip off her clunkers. "They're ugly," she says.

"Like yours are glam."

She's wearing argyle socks. Thick and bulky. As she yanks them up, the heel rises halfway to her calf. Men's socks. Her feet swim in them. Her feet are tiny, I note. Out of proportion with her body. Of course, I can't really tell how big or small her body is in those baggy clothes. I wonder about her body.

My heart pounds.

She steps into the left shoe, then right, and pushes to stand upright. "Whoa." She wobbles. She has to latch on to a shelving unit behind her to steady herself. She shakes her head and sits again.

"Walk around," I tell her. "They're cushy."

"They're obscene." She removes them slowly, almost lovingly, and presents them to me atop her fleshy palms as if on a royal pillow. "I love them."

What is it with you? I want to ask. What are you? Who are you? You're this powerful, enigmatic creature I don't understand.

She props her elbows on the shelf unit and leans back. It's a competition: Which of us will reveal first? And how much?

"It's definitely heated in here," I say, fanning my face. It must be a hundred and fifty degrees. Fans drone overhead. They're not moving any cool air around, though. Just making noise. Can she feel the heat?

"What did you want to talk about?" she says flatly. "Tam." Every time she opens her mouth it's a surprise. Those lips. Plus, she has a high, lilting voice. I always expect it to be low and masculine. But it's . . . airy.

"Can you believe that guy on our train who rolls around on the skateboard?" I say. "He's, like, cut in half? I mean, he can't help it that he doesn't have legs, but his hair is so gross and filthy it drags on the ground and his fingernails are cracked and they click on the floor. He's missing his thumbs. Did you notice that? God, he creeps me out. Do you even own a coat? I mean, you eat outside every day and I've only ever seen you wear a shirt and vest. On the train too. Did anyone tell you it was winter? The temperature drops. It snows. I guess the socks are warm they look warm."

Shut up, Tam, I think. You're revealing. "I'm sorry," I say, spreading open my hands in a helpless gesture. "It's a sickness."

She laughs. She actually lowers her head and chuckles.

Now I'm wondering, Is she laughing at me?

Then she says, "That guy is my uncle Ralph."

I gasp a little.

She raises her head and her eyes gleam.

Kill her. How do I know when she's joking?

A smile sits on her lips. I want to ask about the lipstick so bad. Not yet.

"What do people call you?" I ask again. "I know your name's Andrea. But does anyone call you that?"

"All my multitudes of friends," she says. "My armies and legions of fans." She doesn't take her eyes off me.

I don't let her go there. "What do you want me to call you? If you can lower your standards to let me in your army."

She exhales, like this conversation takes effort. "Whatever you want to call me. Tam."

We let that moment pass.

It's so damn hot. Sweat trickles down my hairline to my chin. I swipe it away with the back of my thumb.

"You could take something off," she suggests, a lewd grin creeping across her lips. "If you're hot."

"Good idea." I stand and pull my sweatshirt over my head. I start to unbutton my shirt, but she holds up a hand.

"Please. I just ate lunch."

I knew she'd be sarcastic. I just knew it.

"You're different in person," she says out of nowhere.

What'd she mean "in person"? She sees me every day.

I knew what she meant. I wasn't "in character." Wasn't doing my act, playing my role. Being "Tamlyn." I was beginning to despise Tamlyn, Tam, the good girl, the predictable girl. The girl who knew the rules and margins. She never strayed outside the boundaries of accepted behavior. She never stretched the limits.

I hate my own limits. I hate that I judge people, label people. I hate that I'm no better than anyone else. I want to be better.

Even more, I want to be free. Of restrictions and confines

and suffocating expectations. There's more to me than meets the eye. I want her to know that. I *need* her to know.

"Yeah, well," I say to her. "You're different too. Andrea."

Her eyes fall. I think I've insulted her.

"I mean you're easy to talk to."

Her head flops to the side.

"Serious. You should talk to people more. Let them in." Puncture the skin, I think. Peel back the layers. I should talk. "You don't make it easy."

She snipes, "Yeah? Well, neither do you."

I feel like I've been punched.

She says more quietly, "Talk to who? Who wants in?"

"I do." A beat passes. I take a breath and look at her. "I've been dying to get in."

She arches her eyebrows, like, Whoa. Too much information. I don't take it back because it's the truth. It's time.

"You'll be sorry."

I frown and hold her gaze. "Why?"

She swallows. After a pause she replies, "You'll be disappointed with what you find. Or what you're expecting to find."

That softens me. "You don't know that." She opens her mouth to say something else, but I add, "Anyway, I get to decide."

She shakes her head at the floor. What? The conversation stalls. I don't want it to end here. "Can I tell you something about myself? Something personal? Promise you won't laugh."

She doesn't answer.

"My greatest fear is that I'll die alone. Not that I'll die, but that I'll be alone at the end. Unloved." Okay, that was a revelation, even to me.

I think I see her head nod. "My greatest fear?" She glances up at me sideways. "Is that I'll *live* alone. My whole life. That it's always going to be this way."

Do her eyes well? She gets up suddenly and grabs her pack. I reach out to snag her, but she's headed for the door.

"You won't," I say at her back. "It doesn't have to be." Reach out, I think. You have to reach out.

The bell rings, reverberating off the walls and heater vents and fans. We both cover our ears until the echo dies down. She turns slightly and our eyes meet. I see just beyond the outline of her, to the aura of her. It's blue.

Blue is my favorite color.

"We should go," she says. "We don't want to get locked in here overnight."

I shoulder my pack.

"Can you imagine us having a conversation that long?"

I answer, "As a matter of fact, I can. It'd be interesting."

She smiles at that. She opens the door and a whoosh of cold air blows in from the hallway. We both suck it up. She holds the door and I start out ahead of her. "Hey." I turn back. "Can I ask you a question?"

"There doesn't seem to be any stopping you," she says.

I curl a lip at her. Then seriously, "Why the lipstick?"

She just looks at me.

"Really. It just seems so . . ."

"Out of character?" Wide grin. Knowing grin.

Yeah, okay. I get it. She wants people to wonder. She wants someone, anyone, to ask.

Since I did, does she see there's more to me?

We walk down the hall a ways. "Andi," she says out of nowhere. "With an *i*."

"What?" I stop to let a clique of people pass. My group. Becca, who starts talking to me.

I don't hear a word. I run after *her*.

She must hear my clunky shoes. "Andi." She twists her head over her shoulder. "Call me Andi."

"Okay." I come astride her. "Andi."

"Tam." She nods once and smiles. "I'm glad to know you."

We stand close for an instant, a blitz of time. Life goes on around us. The late bell rings and we have to separate. Andi heads off in one direction, me in another. I pivot and call back to her, "Andi."

She spins around.

"Save me a seat on the train."

Can't Stop the Feeling

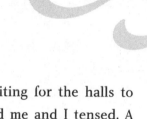

I stalled around at my locker waiting for the halls to clear. Footsteps sounded behind me and I tensed. A body blurred past. No one I knew. My heart drummed as I walked toward the arts wing.

Keep moving, Mariah. Keep going.

I pulled the crinkled newspaper from my pack. Checked the time, like it'd changed.

Every week when *The Bugle* came out, I'd snatch one from the bin and slip it into my spiral. At night I'd read and re-read it. Not the whole thing; it was boring. The notice on back: GSA MEETINGS, THURSDAY 3:00, BAND ROOM 2.

GSA. Gay/Straight Alliance. Just seeing the word on the page made me cold.

There it was. Band Room 2. The door was closed. I passed it, shivering, and impaled myself on the wall at the far end of the corridor. My chest hurt. I checked my watch. 3:10. It was too late. I'd make a scene with my entrance.

I didn't have to do this. You don't have to, Mariah, I told myself. There's always next Thursday. Next week, next year to hide, to lie, to hate yourself.

Someone was coming. In a panic, I charged into the girls' restroom. Blocked the door until they passed. Slamming my pack to the floor, I curled into a ball beside the sink and hugged my knees. I buried my head. Damn. Dammit! The floor was filthy; the pipes reeked of mold. I reeked of cowardice.

A toilet flushed overhead and the gurgle of water in the drain next to my ear registered as E flat, G sharp. . . . I raised my head. Stupid.

This was so weak. I drew a deep breath and let it out slowly. Calmer. Okay. I wasn't going. I was safe. For another week.

Band Room 2. What a weird place to hold a meeting. Especially this kind of meeting. I'd spent most of my life in band rooms. I'd been in band since elementary school. Not too many people stayed with band — not as long as I did. A lot of the girls dropped out our freshman year because they didn't want to be known as "band geeks." Band geeks don't get guys, they said. Whatever.

I played clarinet. Not great, just good enough. In middle school I picked up sax and trumpet. This year, for marching band, I was trying tuba. I'd been in enough band rooms I could walk into one blindfolded and identify the smells: rosin, oil, spit, sweat.

At the moment all I smelled was the stench of my own yellow belly.

It was October already. Five Thursdays, come and gone. Five GSAs. I promised myself this year, my sophomore year, I'd do it. I'd push past the fear. My skull thunked against the drainpipe. Lower C. I squeezed my eyes closed.

If anyone saw this — how I spent every Thursday after school — they'd lock me up. They'd call me chickenshit. That was better than what I'd be called if I got caught at a Gay/Straight Alliance meeting.

Pervert. Queer. Dyke.

My throat tightened. I clunked my head over and over. What was wrong with me? I was wrong. *It* was wrong.

I don't know when it started. Three p.m. Not the meeting. The feelings. Sixth grade? Seventh? They wouldn't stop. Hard as I tried, the feelings wouldn't go away. I'd see girls in class or in the hall and my eyes would latch on to them and my heart would flutter. I'd imagine us alone, at my house, or hers, at the movies, in the dark. Kissing. Touching.

Banish the thought.

All my friends were dating, but I had no interest in guys. How could that be? Why me?

I knew there were others like me. Right down the hall in Band Room 2.

The restroom door flew open and I scrambled to my feet. This girl stopped and did a double take. Her eyes flitted around the stalls, then back to me. "Are you okay?"

I swallowed hard and choked out, "Yeah."

"Sure?"

No! I screamed inside. I'm dying. Can't you see? Can't everybody see what I am? Snatching up my backpack, I raced out the door.

∞

End of the world. That's what it felt like. I couldn't be gay. It was against everything I knew, everything I believed.

Every day it built up. Day after day after day. The feelings, the confusion. The loneliness. I'd be talking to my friends and they'd say something like, "That is so gay." Or, "She's such a dyke." Or, "Can you imagine kissing a girl?" Can I imagine it? I dreamt about it.

In my dreams I was happy, whole. I was me. No one cared that I liked girls. I didn't have to keep up this charade or squelch this giant secret that was killing me inside.

I didn't have to. You don't, Mariah. You're not gay.

If I didn't acknowledge the feelings, I wouldn't have to face the fact.

The fact that I was gay.

I tried not to think about it so much. But it was like this

constant buzz in my ear, this sour note rising in pitch and volume, making me want to scream.

∞

Thursday again. Thermonuclear Thursday. All week I'd worked on concocting a story. In case I worked up the courage to actually go. I would go. I swore to myself, this was the week. I rationalized, it was the Gay/Straight Alliance, right? I could be straight. The story was — if anyone asked, if I got as far as stepping foot into Band Room 2 at three on Thermonuclear Thursday — that I forgot my instrument. "Sorry to interrupt. I'll just get my instrument." Stall around. See what it was like. Go. Or stay. Today after jazz band I left my clarinet in Band Room 2. Accidentally on purpose.

I wasn't good at lying. I hated lying. I could live without my clarinet for one night. My first clarinet, the one I got when I was eight, was at home in the hall closet. Two keys stuck and the reed was a hundred years old, but I could still practice. I could compensate for its weaknesses.

Sure, Mariah. Who would compensate for yours?

There was the door.

Here it came. That physical dread and a sense of doom that made me sick. And weak. No reason to risk being discovered. No reason at all.

The door was closed. I was late. They'd notice me coming in.

They'd see me coming out. Coming out.

Was I coming out?

How did people do this? It was too hard.

Bad plan. I should've arrived early so I could check out who was in the GSA. What if there were people I knew?

Not likely. I didn't know anyone gay. Or even questioning. If only I did. If someone would come with me, support me, hold me up when my knees were buckling because I couldn't even stand at the door long enough to open it, and I couldn't stand myself for being such a coward.

My stomach cramped. What if people saw me coming out? Of the meeting, I mean. They'd tag me. Even if I was a straight supporter, it'd be all over school by morning. Mariah's gay. They'd assume. They'd be right. Everyone would look at me. No one would ever talk to me again. Or they'd ask, "Are you?"

No. I could never admit it out loud. All I knew was this need. To be free. To be me.

The door was a heartbeat away. My knees and hands began to shake.

Without commanding it, my arm raised. My fingers curled around the doorknob and I felt my chest constrict with the pressure. My blood went cold. I didn't have to do this. Don't, Mariah. Don't!

Click. Push.

Laughter spilled out of the room. People, twelve or fifteen, were sprawled on the stage or straddling chairs or sitting on desks. They stopped laughing.

Heads swiveled. I froze. Every bone in my body went brittle. I couldn't move, couldn't breathe. There was a prolonged, grave silence.

"Hi." The tinny sound echoed in my head. Hi. A death knell. I tried to step back, out, reverse the action.

The spotlight was on me. I shriveled in place. That's why I loved being in band. Because I didn't stand out; I was part of a group. I needed to blend.

Unexpectedly, the smell of rosin hit me and all my muscles relaxed.

"You looking for the GSA?"

"What?" Did that squeak come from me?

"GSA. I just figured out, that's Girl Scouts of America," a guy said. "We should sell cookies."

"You've already given all your cookies away," another guy quipped. A few people went "Oooh" and howled.

They'd laugh at me. They already were. I stumbled backward.

"Come in. You're welcome here." A man stood. Teacher, I thought. Or counselor. I'd seen him around. He had a red beard.

"No, I . . ." This was a mistake. This wasn't the way.

A girl, cross-legged on the stage, bounded to her feet and brushed off her jeans. I'd seen her. In the restroom last Thursday. Before that, though. In the halls, the cafeteria, on the bleachers during games. She'd registered on my radar. Gaydar? Was there such a thing?

She approached me with her hand extended. "Hi. I'm Lily."

"Um . . . no." I reached behind me for the doorknob.

She arched her eyebrows.

"I mean, I'm just here to get my instrument." My heart thrummed.

Smiling, Lily dropped her arm. "Okay." Our eyes met and locked. For an instant I thought, Possibility?

No. Impossibility.

She said, "Do I know you?"

I shook my head real fast. You don't know me. No one knows.

She seemed to clue in. "What instrument do you play?" she asked casually.

"What instrument do you play?" a mocking voice sang behind Lily.

Lily whirled. "Shut up." She turned back to me and rolled her eyes. "Sorry. Asstards." She smiled again.

I might've smiled back. My face was so tight I thought it'd split. I was clutching my backpack to my chest and feeling the crushing weight in my lungs. Instinctively, my field of vision expanded to take in everyone again. Thank God they were strangers. Except the two guys at the far end of the stage. Oh my God! I knew them from band.

In a soft voice Lily said, "You don't have to be afraid."

"I'm not," I said, clenching my backpack in a death grip. "I just came to get my . . . my clar . . . clar —"

Lily's eyes widened.

". . . inet." My voice cracked.

"So," she tilted her head, "where is it?"

"What?"

Lily laughed. She had this bubbly, infectious laugh that made me want to laugh. Maybe I did, a little. "Duh," I went.

The storage room was behind the stage. The drummer, he was looking at me now. Nailed. Might as well . . . "I'll just get . . ." I lifted a limp finger and Lily swiveled to look in the direction I was pointing. I ducked my head and skittered around her, across the stage floor. The other guy, Ace or Trace, had rolled onto his stomach. He'd only joined band at the beginning of this year. He hitched his chin off the back of his hands and said, "Hiya."

I blew out a breathy "Hi."

"Woodwinds, right?"

My shoulders hunched. A bleak smile might've stretched across my lips.

The storeroom was locked. Damn. But I knew it would be. I cursed under my breath. Make a show of it. My rehearsed lie. I wheeled around.

A conversation on the other side of the room had resumed without me, in spite of me. Good acoustics in here. Great. A guy was talking about coming out to his family, how his mom did this whole drama scene, sobbing at the dinner table and accusing him of ruining her life. How his dad offered to hire him a prostitute. Everyone groaned at that.

I did not even want to go there. Telling my family? I couldn't imagine what Mom would do. She'd go ballistic. Dad?

The dread and fear of exposing myself to them was nothing compared to telling my friends. Did they even qualify as friends? There wasn't one of them I could trust, or confide in.

Lily must've seen how green I got because she piped up, "My mom was fine with it. My dad too. I mean, not everyone has a bad experience coming out."

"That's true," another girl said. "For me it was like this huge relief not to have to hide anymore. Or lie."

Hide and lie.

"It's always a relief," one of the guys said. "Every time you come out."

You had to do it more than once? I guess he meant to your family, then your friends. Ex-friends. Friends who'd find you disgusting. Sick.

Once would be enough. Once was too much.

Ace said, "So are you . . . ?"

I couldn't do this. I ran for the exit.

"Hey," Lily called behind me. "Wait." A wall, the restroom, a bank of lockers flew by. "What's your name?"

I ground to a stop. My whole body was shaking. My balance was rocky, but I braced and turned around.

"Mariah," I said. My voice sounded raspy. Dry throat. "Mariah Morales."

"Mariah." She crossed her arms loosely and let them fall. Like she was nervous. *She* was nervous? "You can stay," she said. "You're welcome."

"No." I shook my head. "I can't."

She held my eyes for a moment, then nodded. I didn't want her to feel sorry for me. But she smiled warmly, like she understood. "When you're ready," she said. Her voice was steady, and sure.

She took a step back, pivoted, and left me there.

I watched as she strode down the hall, as she disappeared back into the band room.

It was quiet, no noise. No screaming or yelling or running in the halls. No fear, no dread. Just peace. It lingered.

When I'm ready, Lily had said. My eyes lit on Band Room 2. The door was left open.

After Alex

Rachael, I fucked up. I know that.
I'm sorry. I need you.
Please, Rach. I want you back.
<3 Alex

I showed Jordan the printout and her eyes slit as she scanned the page. "She can't be serious," Jordan said. "She wants you *back*?"

Teva crooked her neck to read from Jordan's lap. She screwed up her face. "God. She is such a player."

"No, she isn't," I said.

"Rachael." Jordan cocked her head at me.

My eyes fell. They dredged across the checkered floor. Peeling tiles and crud in the corner. Jamba Juice had aged a hundred years. Had I been out of it that long?

"Rachael," Jordan said.

I lifted my eyes slowly.

"She is."

No, she isn't, I argued to myself. She isn't. She only loves me.

Teva took a sip of her smoothie. "You're not thinking about going back with her, are you?"

I bent to my straw. No. I wasn't.

Jordan dug out a lighter from her purse and flicked it, then set the corner of the printout on fire.

"Jordan!" Teva and I cried together. "God." Teva laughed. She grabbed the paper and flung it to the ground. "You're a pyro." She stomped it.

Jordan watched the paper curl, eyes glazing over. "Fire is life," she said vacantly. Teva's eyes met Jordan's, catching fire. The heat between them made my throat close.

My mind shifted to Alex's words, her letter. Sitting in the dark reading her e-mail over and over. *I need you. I want you back.* How long had I waited to hear those words? *I need you.* Missing her. *I want you.* Wanting her desperately. If it wasn't for Jordan and Teva dragging me out of my room occasionally, I'd shrivel up and die. I wanted to.

The constant presence of Alex in my life, the notes and calls and nights and weekends together. Being together. Alex and Rachael. We were a couple. Her arm around my shoulders, my waist, her holding my hand, holding me. Kissing me, steering me into a restroom for a couple of minutes alone together before class. Her hand sliding up the front of my shirt. Not caring about getting caught, or being known.

That was Alex. She loved me. She loved me for all the world to see.

"We hate Alex," Jordan said, dropping her lighter back into her bag.

"Yeah," Teva went. "After what she did to you? We hate her."

I hate her too. No, I don't. I hate what she did.

Alex came out when she was thirteen. At seventeen, two years into it, I was still struggling. I was gay, yeah. A lesbian, no question. It was just harder for me. Telling Mom. My friends. Mom didn't believe it. She said, "How do you know? You can't know. You're only fifteen." Yes, Mother. You know at fifteen. You know at twelve, thirteen. You look at girls and you know. You sit next to them in class and you feel it. The attraction, the desire. You hold it inside because you're afraid of it, afraid of what it means. You never tell anyone. You hope it goes away. You hope it doesn't mean what you know it does.

Mom didn't believe I was gay. Not until Alex.

Mom liked Alex right away. Alex is easy to like. I mean, she was. She gave off this joie de vivre. She laughed, joked, mimicked people. She had Teva down, how Teva sort of waddled when she walked. It was funny. Kind of mean. Alex practically lived at our condo.

It was easier for Alex. Maybe because she got there sooner, came out to herself, she was more comfortable with it. The whole idea of being gay, being different. Her fuck-you-if-you've-got-a-problem-with-it attitude. People respected her. I did. She had thick skin and red blood. When Alex began to skip the restroom and kiss me in the hall — do other stuff — I showed my skin. I pushed her away.

She said, "What's the matter, Rach? Don't you love me?"

Of course I loved her. I just . . . I didn't want people . . . ogling. Or sniggering behind our backs. I told her that.

"Who gives a fuck?" Alex had said.

I did. I don't know, it made me feel weird. It hurt my feelings to be called names.

"They'll destroy you," Alex told me. "If you let them control you, they'll fuck with your head. You give them power over you, Rachael."

Yeah, I did. I hated myself for it.

"You can't live your life trying to please other people."

I don't. I do.

∞

It was Thanksgiving weekend and we were riding home on the train from Winter Park. A ski trip. I'd finally gotten up the nerve to join the Gay/Straight Alliance at school, after Jordan's pressuring. Not pressuring. Encouraging. People were quiet on the train, dozing. It'd been an awesome day of skiing. A long day, though. I'd been up since five a.m. to rent equipment and have Mom drive me downtown to the ski train. She and Dad had had a fight on the phone the night before about child support or something and she was ragging on me about how expensive this trip was and how we both needed to make sacrifices. Major guilt trip. A whole day on the slopes, carting my skis and poles around, forgetting sunblock and searing my nose and forehead. I knew I'd blister and peel. A two-hour train ride back to Denver.

I wasn't sleepy, the way I normally was after skiing. I was wide awake, alert. Whenever Alex was near, I felt that way. Tingly. Wired. She'd come with her girlfriend, Courtney.

Courtney.

Jordan was conked out next to me and I was resting my temple on the window to watch the trees streak by in the dark, to think. About Alex, four rows ahead. How she'd smiled at me as I'd boarded the train and held my eyes as I'd weaved down the aisle past her. How she'd clung to me. Not physically. Psychically.

Courtney wasn't with Alex. She'd stormed down the aisle and plopped into a rear bench seat. They'd had a fight or something.

The cold window penetrated my skull and made me shiver all over. I scooted out around Jordan to grab a blanket from the overhead bin. She flopped over onto my seat. You can't wake Jordan up if you beat her with a ski boot.

I scanned over the high seat backs for an empty row. The train was pretty full, but there was a double seat up front. In my moon boots, I clunked up the aisle and scooted over to sit next to the window. As I was unfolding the blanket across my lap, I heard beside me, "God, it's freezing in here. Mind if I share?"

She didn't wait for an answer, just sank down next to me and pulled a corner of the blanket over her lap, tucking it under her thigh. Our shoulders touched. She snuggled up close. My breath caught and my blood pulsed. Could she feel me trembling? Her knee nudged mine and I almost cried out. Maybe I did a little. She twisted her head and smiled.

She billowed the blanket over our heads and leaned into me. "I thought we'd never be alone," she whispered.

"I know," I whispered back. I couldn't believe I said that. How fast it all happened.

We giggled. We fooled around. Then . . .

She kissed me. That kiss. It was light, at first. Questioning. My answer: Yes. Oh yes. Like an avalanche rolling and roaring to life, picking up speed, volume, intensity, power, the momentum carried me away.

Alex was cool. Amazing. And unavailable.

Courtney.

I didn't want to think about Courtney.

We were meant to be, Alex and me. We were tight.

∞

But that was then. This was now. After Alex.

My life was defined by three eras:

Before Alex.

During Alex.

After Alex.

Sad, happy, miserable.

"You want to share?" Jordan said.

"What?"

She wasn't talking to me. She and Teva slid their smoothies together and pinched their straws at the top so they could sip and kiss at the same time.

I turned to stare out the window. There was life after Alex. There was.

The first time is intense, that's all. You never forget your first.

The first time we made love was on a Friday afternoon. I had a test in biology, but Alex said I could make it up. The way she looked at me, touched my face.

We did it on the living room sofa wrapped in Mom's afghan. Mom took up crocheting after Dad left. Crocheting and crabbing at me. She was at work that day. Afterward, Alex was propped on her elbow, combing her fingers through my tangled hair. "Rach," she said softly, lovingly, "you're so good to me."

"You're good to me," I said. "You're good for me."

She smiled. "Yeah. I am."

I lived to please her.

I don't anymore.

"Rachael?" Fingernails dug into my arm. "You okay?" Jordan asked.

I blinked at her. Where was I? Jamba Juice. Alex's e-mail.

I need you. I want you back.

The stirring in my stomach.

"It'd be like one of those abusive relationships where the wife or girlfriend always goes back to the asshole who's smacking her around because he says he's *sorree*," Teva mocked. Her head bobbed on her shoulders, braids clacking. Her fiery eyes flared.

What was she talking about?

"Or some guy who cheats on his wife," Jordan added. "She just forgives and forgets."

No, I thought. It's not the same.

Alex wasn't abusive. She was good to me. Good for me. She was gentle and loving. It wasn't cheating. It was . . . forgiveness. She afforded people every opportunity they deserved. Courtney deserved it.

Courtney's face flashed through my mind. That Monday after the ski trip when I found her in the locker room, crying. I had nothing to do with it. It wasn't my fault. Alex and Courtney were already over; that's what Alex said. They were always fighting. Alex never talked about what happened between them, only that they needed a break. They'd been together for more than a year. Off and on.

Courtney was needy, Alex said. Alex felt smothered by her.

"What makes women do that?" Teva asked, bending to sip from her straw. "Do they like pain? Do they enjoy it?" Her smoothie gurgled.

"They don't think they can get anyone else," Jordan said, lighting a cigarette. "They have no sense of self-worth." She drew in a long drag and blew out the smoke. "They're victims. But they do it to themselves."

I watched the stream of smoke dissipate in the air.

Teva swallowed and shook her head. "You have to really hate yourself to let someone hurt you that way. And keep hurting you."

They both fixed on me. Not too subtle. Yeah, Alex had hurt me; she'd hurt me bad. But it wasn't the same. She'd never hit me. We never fought. She was always kind and giving. "I love you, Rachael," she'd said. "I love you with all my heart."

"Rachael?"

I shook my head at Jordan. You're wrong.

The counter clerk stormed over. "No smoking in here."

Jordan blinked up at her. She scanned the length of her. Sucking in another drag, Jordan blew smoke in the girl's face. Then dropped the cigarette into her glass.

It hissed.

I sipped from my smoothie, remembering Courtney. She smoked. I'd see her out smoking at the wall, alone. Or crying. I released my mind of conscious thought and allowed in only sensory stimuli. Sensuous feeling. Alex kissing me. On my lips, my neck, my breasts.

Heat swelled my skin.

Jordan kicked my foot. "Rachael, she can't be trusted." Her eyes penetrated my soul.

"I know." Trust is crucial.

Alex's words clawed their way to the surface. "It just happened, Rach. I didn't mean for it to happen. We ran into each other at the mall and started talking and I realized how much I missed her. How I still loved her."

The searing pain. My heart ripping, being torn from my chest.

"I don't *not* love you," she'd added.

I'm not sure where I found the strength to speak. "But you love her more," I'd said. Stated for the record.

She didn't confirm or deny. I wanted to scream, What about how needy Courtney is? How she smothers you?

You love me with all your heart, remember? I love you with all my soul.

I'd whimpered to myself, I don't smother you. I only do what you want. I even let you grope me in public.

I should've said it. I know that now. Not the groping part. The Courtney part.

It was Courtney I wanted to smother. Hold a pillow over her face until she was dead. God, I'm so horrible.

"Alex," I'd pleaded. "Please." Please, I'd begged for my life. Pleeeeease.

She'd taken my hand. "Rach, if you love me, let me go. Let me do what I need to do. Don't make it hard."

Hard? Try excruciating.

To my credit, I didn't bawl in front of her. No drama. I loved her that much. I didn't make it hard.

No. She couldn't expect me to take her back. After she dumped me — "Rach, do this for me. Don't make it hard" — I cut. Alone, in the bathroom. It hardly bled. No surprise. I couldn't even cut right.

It took practice.

"Oh my God." Jordan glanced at her watch. "We have to go." She scraped back her chair and stood. "The mall's closing in fifteen minutes and I have to buy my dad a birthday present."

Teva stood with Jordan. She took the hand Jordan offered her. "You want to come with us?" Teva asked.

I shook my head no. No, no, no. I hated the mall now. I hated being the third wheel.

Jordan touched my shoulder.

"I'm okay," I said, peering up at her. Smiling. "I'll call you later."

Jordan tugged the lip of my baseball cap over my face. She and Teva left. Jordan paused outside on the sidewalk and pressed her hand to the glass. I waved. I was happy for her; glad she and Teva had finally hooked up. They were perfect. There was trust and respect between them.

I walked home in the dark. Remembering the mountains, the blur of trees, the kiss. At the condo complex, I clunked up the stairs to the second floor. The words Teva'd left me with echoed in my head. "Forget her, Rachael. Alex doesn't deserve you. She never was good enough for you."

How many times had I heard that? From Teva, Jordan.

"She's not good enough for you, Rachael. You're such a good person. You deserve better."

What we deserve and what we get are two different things.

∞

It was cold in the condo. I punched up the thermostat. Mom was working the night shift again. That's what Alex loved about coming over, the time we got alone. "This is what it'll be like when we're together forever," she'd said. "In our own place."

There was never any doubt. "I love you with all my heart."

I lay on the sofa and pulled Mom's afghan over me, remembering. Alex's touch, her smell. She always smelled like baby powder. I remember the feel of her body fitted up against mine, her playing with my belly ring, tickling me. Giggling. Goofing around. Getting serious.

The ache. The physical ache of her being gone, being with Courtney. Doing with her what we did together.

I crunched into a ball.

How Courtney had come around the corner and almost run into me sitting on the bench in the locker room on Thursday. I was just sitting, staring into space. How shocked she was to see me. How happy she was to be back with Alex.

I saw my happiness in her eyes. The only time I'd been truly happy in my life. Courtney stole that from me. It wasn't

Alex's fault that she'd forgiven Courtney and taken her back. I bet Courtney begged. I bet she cried; she made it hard for Alex.

Alex would've remembered how manipulative Courtney was. How needy and suffocating. How love is more than giving, giving, giving. It's forgiving too.

How much can you forgive? How many times? There's a point where you have to say no. No more. I have no more to give.

I threw back the afghan and padded to my bedroom, to my computer. I pressed the On button. The monitor lit up and the drive whirred to life. I retrieved Alex's e-mail.

I'd deleted the last part of the message before printing it off to show Jordan and Teva. *She's so needy,* Alex had written. *You should've reminded me why I broke up with her in the first place. I swear, Rachael, Courtney sucks the life out of a person. You never did that to me. You feed me. You nourish me.*

Then why? Why, Alex? You had to know what it would do to me to lose you. I'd starve to death. I did. You left me emptied.

Rachael, I fucked up. I know that. I'm sorry. I need you.

No, Alex. Don't make it hard.

Please, Rach. I want you back.

I can't. My heart hammered in my chest.

I stared at the screen, at the words. I felt myself ripping in half, as if my body was separating from my soul.

I keyed in one word.

"Okay."

Outside/Inside

I won't sign the card, I decided. I'll let her wonder who it's from.

No. I wanted her to know. I wanted her to look at me every day and know.

There were so many cards to choose from. Christmas, New Year, Hanukkah, Kwanzaa, Birthday. None of them fit. Friendship?

Yes. Well, no. Not exactly.

Thank you?

No.

Love? Yes, that was the kind of card I wanted.

(Outside) I love you

(Inside) Every day/In every way

That was true. I loved her in every way. A little heavy on the sentiment, though. Smack her in the face.

(Outside) My day begins

(Inside) With you

It did. First period. I couldn't wait to get to school to see her first period. Sometimes I'd catch her in the hallway before class, talking to people and smiling. Always smiling. She was my happy, smiling sunshine.

There's a song like that. Were there cards with song lyrics? I could make one.

(Outside) You are my sunshine

(Inside) My only sunshine

Dorky. What's the rest? You make me happy, when skies are gray. She did. It could be raining or snowing outside and the sight of her would light up the halls.

She dressed cool. Not sexy or provocative. Except this one time she'd worn a scoop-neck sweater and she was sitting on the steps outside the cafeteria after lunch, and I remember she leaned back to tilt her face to the sun. I'd just come out the door with my friends to head for the quad so they could check out guys. I was standing a couple of steps above her and she inhaled a deep breath and her breasts heaved. I could see down her front, to the trim of her bra. I must've gasped or something because her head lolled all the way back and she said, "Hi." To all of us, yeah. But in particular to me. I was so startled by the view I almost took a header down the steps.

That would've been a trip.

(Outside) You had me at

(Inside) Hi

I wondered if she'd get it; recall that day. And every other day she said hi to me.

(Outside) Imagine

(Inside) Us together

I did. All the time. I fantasized about us together. Standing under a trellis, ivy dripping down the sides. Her, in her white wedding gown with scooped neck and lace-trimmed bra, and me, in my tuxedo. Black silk, black shirt, black tie. She'd be holding a bouquet of red roses. Black and white and red. Those would be our colors. We'd vow eternal love and consummate it with a kiss. Our first kiss.

(Outside) Your lips on mine

(Inside) I shiver

Oh wow. I liked that one. It was simple, yet strong. Boldly suggestive.

As the guy at the counter rang up my sale, he said, "I got that same one for my girlfriend."

"Yeah?" I'm getting it for mine, I didn't say. My 2B GF.

I had a red glitter pen and a green Flair, but decided to go with black gel. Sophistication. I wanted her to think of me that way. Red, white, and black.

Your lips

On mine

I shiver

Hoo. This card made me hot. Print or write my message? Write, I decided. On a sheet of notebook paper, I practiced the lettering: *L L L L L L.*

Three lines of *L*'s.

Commit, I thought.

Love, I wrote. I wrote it again.

Love.

Love, Logan.

I closed the card and kissed the red foil heart on front. I'd leave her my lip print. My hands were clammy as I slid the card into the envelope, sealed it, and wrote her name on the front. My finest writing. It'd be hard, but I'd force myself to wait until Friday to give it to her. Last day before winter break. Give her something to think about during those two weeks. Someone to think about.

Maybe I should've put my phone number under my name.

Right, Logan. Don't be too obvious.

She could look me up. Or ask me for it when we got back from break. It'd sustain me to know she was thinking about me.

She snapped to attention when I approached her desk, like she'd been lost in thought. I'd waited until after class. Until she'd begun to gather her stuff. Her face lit up. "Hi, Logan."

"Hi."

She smiled. Her smile extended to her eyes. From your eyes to my heart, I thought. Without even knowing her that well, I could see she had a beautiful soul. Before I lost my nerve, I pulled the card from my math book and handed it to her.

She read the front. "For me?"

Did she blush? She flipped over the envelope and stuck a fingernail under the flap.

"Youcanopenitlater," I said in a rush.

She paused. "All right." She smiled again. "Are you taking AP English next term?"

"Yeah," I said.

"I'm glad." She dropped her eyes.

The late bell rang.

"Oops, better fly." She slipped my card into her shoulder bag.

"Yeah, me too," I said. Fly.

She hurried toward the door. "Have a happy holiday, Logan," she called over her shoulder.

"Yeah." I stood in her afterglow, warm as the sun. I called to her back, "You too, Ms. Winger."

On the Floor

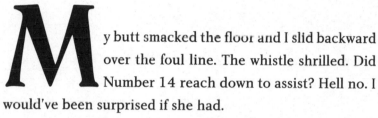

My butt smacked the floor and I slid backward over the foul line. The whistle shrilled. Did Number 14 reach down to assist? Hell no. I would've been surprised if she had.

Right in my face, she exaggerated a grin. Baited me. Then she swaggered back to her team's bench. Girl, I thought, streaking a silent message across court, watch your ass tonight. Someone extended a hand and yanked me up.

Her team, the Wombats, was already in foul trouble. Thanks to her. Ref flipped me the ball. I dribbled once, then rotated the skin around between my open palms. It was second skin to me. I'd been shooting hoops with my brothers since I could walk. By the time I was ten, I was beating the crap out of them. It was height, yeah, but instinct too. I was born to it.

My toe caps leveled the foul line. I shadowed the stripe.

Microscopic advantage, if anyone dared to measure. I sighted the net, then rocked back on my right heel and gripped the ball; squared my elbows, gentled the leather, talked the ball in; made love to it; released.

Hahhhh . . . An owl swooping through the forest at night. It sights the prey, dives in for the KILL.

Muffled cheering from the crowd.

Barracudas up by three.

I glanced sideways to my left, to check her reaction. She bent over her haunches and tugged at the hem of her shorts. Long, sculptured legs. Hard, like mine. 14 flexed, and her quads rippled sweat.

At the catch in my lower stomach I exhaled a swift breath. Focus. Don't get distracted.

Bonus shot. I dribbled once and spun the ball around in my hands. Calloused palms. Tentacled fingers. As I loaded for release, urging my baby on, 14 straightened suddenly in her stance and twisted her head to bore eyes into me. I couldn't help looking. She smiled big white teeth.

My shot sailed left. *Chunk.* It clipped the rim. Damn. Damn her. It bounced up and out.

The Wombats rebounded and thundered down the court. 14 scudded to a squeaky halt outside the three-point line and reached both hands up for an incoming pass. I cut in front of her and lunged for the ball. My fingertips nicked skin, but she anticipated my move and jockeyed her body sideways into perfect position, snagging the throw. An inch and I would've had it. She spun to shoot, but I planted my feet and mirrored her moves.

She seesawed. I rocked. I windmilled my arms. She passed off over my head to one of her guards, then bumped me hard on the hip, hooking my ankle and tripping me up.

I maintained my balance; stayed with her. We closed in on the basket. In the paint, I muscled under her arm and clipped her in the chest. Wicked elbow. She chuffed. She was taller than me, but I took advantage by seeking out her vulnerable spots — gut, throat, ear. Breasts were off limits, much as I wanted to go there. We played physical, contact. Hard, but not dirty.

She slammed her shoulder into mine and knocked me off point again. The ball arced into her waiting hands. As she laid up her shot, I sprang like a cat and clawed it off course. We both watched it spike in the air and plummet, tipping the backboard. She dove for the rebound, but I got there first and shagged the ball. Squeezing, I caressed the solid mass to my chest.

Charging up the court, lungs filling, feet pounding, sweat spraying, hair flying, ball, skin, heat, friction, driving, diving, dribble, racing down, down. Ball. Up. In.

The game. Play. Bodies clashing, gliding, sliding against each other. Grunting, groaning, crying out. Keening, squealing, primitive animal sounds. The pungent smell, the odor of exertion and exhilaration. The salty taste of sweat — mine and hers. Slick, sticky neck, arms, hands. And always the breathing, huffing, chests expanding. Gorging, groping, cutting, jostling for position. For place, for power. Down, down, deeper, farther. Onto her, into her. Rush.

The rush. We were on. Giving all.

For the game. For play.

We hurtled the space between us; clashing full frontal, we collided and crunched to the floor. We rolled onto each other like wrestlers, soles screeching, stabbing, scrabbling for the ball, knocking arms, heads, bones. Then the ball trickling away out of bounds. The whistle shrilling.

Ref called, "Jump ball." We — 14 and me — we looked at each other and smiled.

Killer smile. She knew the effect.

I got up fast and thrust out a hand. *SLAP,* she grasped it. I yanked.

For a moment she balanced against me, her arm fused to mine. Sizzling skin. Muscle twitch, contraction.

A slit-eyed sideways glance from her.

Yeah, girl. Later. You know it.

We'd meet up, usual spot. Her court. Or mine.

In the darkness we'd play out the game. We'd thrash in the heat and sweat and rush. Didn't matter who won or lost tonight. We were taking this game into overtime.

Stone Cold Butch

"S eriously?" J.J. arched her eyebrows. "You want to go completely bald?"

"Shear it off."

Maybe the transformation wouldn't require excessive mutilation. "Okay, leave some stubble," I said. "Quarter of an inch."

She held up her dog trimmers to my face. "Still time to change your mind."

"Have I ever changed my mind about anything?"

J.J. said, "Could be that's your problem."

"Who says I got a problem?" I snapped at her. "Just shave."

She didn't need to know about my *problem*. There was nothing she could do about my *problem*. Nothing anyone could do. Not J.J., not me, not Taunia.

Taunia.

What did she see in me anyway? I was ugly. Obscene.

Eventually I'd drive her away. I'd have to. I watched in the mirror as J.J. buzzed an arc over my ear. I was hideous. The blotchy skin and zits, my lumpy nose from being broken in a fight, my ears, I noticed at this moment, crooked. There wasn't anything in this mirror, in this person, that Taunia could want.

∞

So why? "Why?" I'd asked her. That day in the hall, after school. After I stomped out of Thatcher's class — bastard — when he refused to give me credit for my project. Because he couldn't understand why I'd chosen to film hunger in America rather than write a report. A boring report on some inconsequential topic. Oh, excuse me. A topic that affected us directly. Hunger affected me, okay. It *affected* me. No, he meant things like the increase in school violence over the last decade. Maybe not inconsequential, but easily explained. It was the anger. Thatcher was the reason for the anger, if you ask me. His indifference. He wouldn't listen. He pissed me off. I didn't want to write my report down because it wasn't about the numbers, facts, words on paper, charts and graphs. You can't understand hunger unless you see it. Unless you feel the weakness and the gnaw in your gut.

"Why what?" Taunia had frowned.

I'd tuned into her voice — her creamy voice — still reeling

from the sting of an F in Sociology. I needed to graduate. Needed to get away from here. "Why would you ask me out?" I sniped at her.

She smiled. "Gee, I don't know. Because I like you?"

Get real. What was there to like?

∞

A clump of hair fell into my lap and J.J. went, "Oops." She sucked air between her teeth. "I got too close. Your brain is exposed."

"Funny."

"It's oozing out."

"Apply pressure," I said.

"It's green. It looks like kryptonite."

"Call Superman."

"It's glomming up my dog shaver. It's swelling to twice its size. It's going to blow. Kaboom!"

"Shut up and shave."

Another clump of hair dropped into my lap.

Now I'd look completely butch. Because I was — strong, powerful, and defiant.

Don't mess with me. I'll take you down.

Sure I will. Big talk.

My thoughts drifted back to yesterday. She'd waited. Taunia. For an answer. Standing there, gazing into my eyes, attempting to hold my attention. So sweet.

A twinge in my belly, then . . . nothing. The dead seeping in. Empty. Hard.

"I can't," I'd told her. I'd walked away.

"Cam." She'd caught up and grabbed my belt loop from behind. "Why? Why won't you go out with me? Don't you like me?"

I'd crimped my eyes closed. Don't let her know, I thought. She'd never understand. "No." Gruff voice. "What made you think I would?"

She'd released her hold on me and stuttered a breath.

Good. I'd hurt her feelings. That'd teach her. That'd show her who she was dealing with. I'd left her there, demolished.

The power fed me.

Then, not three hours later, she called me. "Hi, Cam. Know who this is?" Her voice was all teasing and sexy.

The girl I just pounded into dog meat?

"We don't have to go any place public, you know. We could just, like, meet somewhere and talk."

"Why are you doing this?"

She hesitated. "Doing what?"

I didn't answer. Why didn't she get it?

"I told you, I like you. I want to go out with you and get to know you better. I think you're brave —"

I slammed down the phone. My breathing came in rasps, like an asthma attack. Except I don't have asthma.

"Who was that?" He hollered from the hole, otherwise known as our family room. Family. You'd have to defile the name to call us a family. Families cared about one another. They cherished and respected one another. Families provided safety, security, refuge. I can't remember one day in my whole entire life that I ever felt safe.

"Cammie, who was it?" He bellowed.

"No one," I called through the doorway. "Wrong number. They hung up."

"Come in here," He said.

No. Please no.

My stomach rots. The space around me shrinks and fades. It shrivels gray.

"Cammie?" His voice sugars. "Honey?"

I go, because I have to. He's my Lord and Master.

He's my Father.

"Hey, baby." He coos it. From behind the greasy recliner, I see His hand reach out to me. I clench my teeth. His fingers spread. I place my hand inside His. He squeezes, holds on, leads me around to the front of Him. "Hey." His lips curl up at both ends. It's not a smile. More a leer. "Take down your hair," He says. "You know I like it down."

The bile rises in my throat, but I choke it back. I'm starting to shake. He lets go of my hand and I remove the elastic band from my ponytail. He waggles His index finger for me to lean over. Cupping His hand around the back of my head, He kisses me. On the lips.

The pressure on my head increases. It shifts. Pushing me down. To His lap; to my knees.

I know what's coming. I shut myself off.

Cold. Hard.

"I had a lousy day," He tells me. "My boss is a jerk. One of these days . . .

". . . I wish I had the balls to leave. Just up and quit." He scoots forward. He unzips his pants. "That'd show 'em."

I fade, fade, fade away.

∞

Last night. Last week. Last year. As long as I can remember, back when I was six, eight, before Mom skipped. He never said, "Don't tell." Or if He did I don't remember. No, it was "This is what daddies and their little girls do." It was "Baby, I love you so much. You please me so much."

I wanted to please Him. I had to. He was my father. I knew if I told He'd be mad. They'd take Him away, or me. With Mom gone, I'd have no one at all.

It went on for years. Every night. At first I cried and He'd say, "Shut up. That didn't hurt. If you want me to hurt you, I will. Get on your knees."

Too long, too late. No one could save me now. This is what it is. This is who I am.

Stone. Butch.

Stone cold butch. That's me. Dead. Inanimate. Object. You could take a sledgehammer to me, crack me down the middle, and all you'd find inside would be dirt. You wouldn't want to get your hands dirty. Don't break me.

I needed to be more butch. That was all. I needed the power.

I tried a couple of times to melt the magma. With Reina, my first girlfriend. It was good in the beginning. As long as I did her. But when she wanted to reciprocate, I couldn't. I could not go there. She started getting this need, this mission to bring me. To share in her ecstasy. She wanted it so bad, to love me, that I learned to fake it to make her happy. And it did for a while. It satisfied her. But the deceiving made me feel like shit. Lying together afterward, her telling me how happy it made her that I felt good. Me saying, "I'm glad."

I finally broke it off with Reina; I told her I was doing someone else. Someone better, who could make me come a hundred times faster. That hurt her. It hurt her bad enough she'd never want me back.

Mission accomplished. Then there was this girl at the homecoming dance, the party afterward at someone's house. I was so wasted, she got as far as taking off my bra. I remember watching her as if I was sitting in a dark theater, mesmerized by a movie. A movie starring me. The way her tongue played with my nipple, sucking me into her mouth. I watched from the front row, scene after smoldering scene, flickering across my stone face, my glassy eyes. I felt nothing. Direct stimulation and I couldn't feel a thing. Because what I saw in my movie was Him. Doing it to me.

He ruined me. He turned me into stone.

I let Him.

∞

J.J. and I walked to school and she left me at my locker. Taunia appeared at the end of the hall. She waved at me, like, hi. Here I am if you were looking for me. She was obviously brain-dead. No, she wasn't. She was smart and nice and sexy. She smiled, all hopeful. The thing she was hoping for, I could never deliver.

"I don't give up easily," she said.

That is your fatal flaw, I thought. I tossed my backpack into the bowels of my locker and yanked the skullcap off my head.

Her eyes expanded. "Oh wow," she breathed. "You buzzed it. I love that." Not the reaction I expected. I wanted her to think I was bad, hostile. Same way I need Him to react — to not want to touch me ever again. To be afraid. Because maybe, maybe I looked like a guy now. That would repulse Him. I'd look strong. Able to resist.

She reached up to feel my scalp. I don't know why I let her touch me. I knew I wouldn't feel. "It's soft," Taunia whispered. Her fingertips pressed lightly and she ran her palm along the side of my head, down the back, caressing my ear. Nothing. No shiver of pleasure. I had the most compelling urge to lean into her and let her hold me. Hold me up. Because the crust was crumbling under me and I was disintegrating.

Taunia's face closed in on mine and she said in this sincere voice, "I loved your film. It really spoke to me. I was so moved, Cam. All those sad and hungry people at the soup kitchen, they just made me cry."

My eyes wanted — needed — to fill with water. I wanted the water to spill over and stream down my cheeks and striate my face. I wanted it to furrow a canyon and dig deep into my heart to carve a safe place for her.

But I couldn't. Tears were weak. Tears would be letting go; giving in.

"The way you stood up to Mr. Thatcher. Wow."

Yeah, I thought. Look what it got me.

"Please," she said. "Go out with me once. If you have a terrible time, we don't have to do it again. But you won't. I promise." She touched the tip of my ear. Traced the arc of it. She looked into my eyes.

I summoned all the strength I could muster to match her gaze. She was hopeful. It was the expectation in their eyes I could never resist.

I let out a long breath.

Butch. It didn't mean bastard.

I'd allow her this dream. The movie she saw with a co-starring role. But she'd predict the ending long before intermission. Taunia would find me out. Word would spread.

Cammie is cold. She's a stone cold butch.

Abstinence Makes the Heart Grow Fonder

We had to copy ten reasons off the board why we should practice abstinence.

1. Birth control. The only 100% effective method.

Duh. Any nine-year-old could've figured that one out. Birth control didn't exactly apply to me.

2. Prevent the spread of STDs and HIV.

Okay. Sexually transmitted diseases might be a valid concern. HIV? Not likely. The chances were slim, and not because I wasn't having sex.

3. Personal responsibility and self-control.

Give me a break. Who has self-control?

4, 5, 6: All this moralistic crap about respecting your body and your partner's; protecting your reputation. I respected my body. You had to earn a reputation first, didn't you?

Problem with the abstinence theory was the answer to the question Chad Bennett had asked. He must've used up his one brain cell to formulate an actual intelligent question. "Mrs. Errasco," he said. "What if we don't plan on getting married?"

Chad's clone, Dirk the Jerk, blurted out, "Yeah. What if we're confirmed bachelors, like me and my homeboy Chad here?"

Mrs. Errasco smirked. "You'll be playing a lot of solitaire, won't you?"

Catcalls. Whoops. Dirk whistled. Errasco didn't answer the question. She stood poised with the blackboard eraser in her hand and said, "Do you have these down? There are four more reasons."

I piped up, "Answer the question. Because I'd like to know too."

Mrs. Errasco glared at me. Everyone did. What else is new? She'd hated me from day one when I'd asked if we were going to talk about same-sex stuff in here or if I was just wasting my time with so-called "Sex Ed."

"We're not supposed to do it until marriage, okay?" I repeated. "But what if we're not allowed to *get* married? Like me. How long am I supposed to wait?"

Chad muttered, "Until the cows come home. Mooo."

I spun around and flipped him the bird.

Chad held up his hands defensively.

Errasco ignored us and erased the board.

"I'm serious, Mrs. Errasco. How does this abstinence theory apply to us? Are we never supposed to have sex? Ever?"

She set the eraser in the chalk tray and faced front. The
atmosphere in the room shifted. Desks creaked. A pencil
broke. Minds? Did they shake loose? Doubtful.

"Well, Aimee." Errasco's eyes lit on me. "I guess that's between you and your god."

∞

I stormed out after class. My god? My *god*? What did she
know about my god? She probably thought since I was gay, I
was godless. Against religion. But I'm not. I have a god. I go
to church. My god isn't *her* god. My god doesn't scorn or
condemn me. My god is kind and benevolent and accepting.
We made a sacred pact. I'd be the best person I could be and
God would save me a place in heaven. My heaven. The real
one, where it doesn't matter who you are or how you look or
how you sacrifice your dignity and self-respect most days
just to be true to yourself.

"Aimee, hold up." A person fell into step beside me. "That
was a good question."

My head swiveled. Peyton Faulk? I stopped dead. Peyton
Faulk was talking to me? We used to be best friends. We
carpooled together to school and soccer and gymnastics
and scouts. To swimming lessons, dance lessons until . . .

Until my parents divorced. Until we moved to inner-city housing. Until Peyton stopped talking to me.

You find out who your true friends are. In times of need.

"Errasco's answer was lame. She blew you off." Peyton stuck out her tongue. She had a silver stud that made her look slutty.

"What'd you expect?" I said. "What else could she say?" Don't ask me why I was defending Mrs. Errasco. I didn't need Peyton Faulk defending me.

Peyton said, "I expected her to take your question seriously, at least."

"Yeah, well. It's a big joke. Like me."

I jogged off again and arrived at my locker. As I reached up to spin the dial, Peyton hovered behind me, breathing down my neck. I yanked open the door and backed into her. "What?" I sniped. "Do *you* have an answer? Life sucks. Nothing's fair. Nothing's equal. Your sanctimonious morals don't apply to us." Us — like there was anyone else to defend. I was the only out lesbian at school.

Peyton's face flushed. "That's not . . ." She swallowed hard. "You're right. It isn't fair. It isn't easy for us either. This whole stupid abstinence movement. 'Wait training.' I mean, God. It's unnatural. Biologically. Emotionally. Even spiritually."

"Oh boo hoo, Peyton. You have it so rough." I ground a knuckle into my eye socket. Then thought, Damn. I just smeared my makeup.

Peyton's lips pinched. Her eyes narrowed. "If you weren't

such a bitch, people might actually care about what you thought." She squeaked a pivot and stomped off.

My face stung, like she'd slapped me.

I hate you, Peyton Faulk. I hate people who get to me.

Peyton. It bugged me all day. Her talking to me, opening a dialogue. My pact with God to be a good person. How much dignity do we have to sacrifice to get to heaven?

I hunted Peyton down after school. She was sitting on the retaining wall, joking around with Chad Bennett. I'd seen them hanging out together. She could do better.

Okay, this was going on my Saint Aimee scroll. I summoned courage and swallowed pride.

"So. You guys. What's up?"

Peyton and Chad froze, like freeze-frame. Chad said, "Who's asking?"

Peyton elbowed him in the ribs. He oofed.

"Not much," she replied. "What's up with you?"

Enough chitchat. "I'm glad you're both here," I said. "I wanted to tell you I'm sorry. About being a bitch today in Errasco's class."

Chad eyed me up and down. "What about the rest of the time?"

"Shut up." Peyton fisted his chest. "I'm sorry too," she said to me. "I just wanted to have a conversation with you is all."

Until she'd ambushed me it hadn't even registered that she was in my health class. She was invisible to me. Okay, not entirely. But she inhabited a different dimension. I adjusted the stack of books in my arm and asked, "A conversation about what?"

Peyton's eyes fixed on mine. "Cramps. I get 'em bad with my period and I wanted to know if you had any Midol."

"Ugh." Chad shuddered. "Mature subject matter. Parental guidance suggested." He leapt off the wall and mumbled, "Catch you later, Pey." He took a wide berth around me and swaggered off.

She grinned. "Now that we're rid of him . . ."

There was an awkward silence between us. History. Like how do you break down a barrier that'd been built over time? Reinforced with resentment and anger?

Peyton set her purse on the other side of her and patted the spot Chad had vacated.

She couldn't order me around.

She opened her mouth and curled the tip of her tongue against her teeth. Her stud glistened. She arched her eyebrows. I exhaled surrender. Setting my tower of books on the ledge, I hoisted myself up. Without grunting, I'm proud to say.

"It isn't natural," Peyton said. "We can't ignore our biological urges. We're meant to procreate and carry on the species."

Procreate? "Is Darwin required reading now?"

She just looked at me.

The whole procreation thing made me a little queasy. Just thinking about what guys and girls did together . . . Not the girls so much.

Peyton laughed suddenly. "You should see your face."

I shook my head, a smile twisting my lips.

"I want to have sex," she said.

My jaw unhinged.

She shoved me. "Not with you."

"Thank God."

She laughed.

A cluster of people passed. Peyton's people. Upper crust. They stopped to chat, make arrangements, synchronize their pods. Finally they noticed me polluting their space and dispersed. I waited until they were out of earshot, near the quad, before asking, "Who do you want to have sex with? Not Chad Bennett, I hope."

Peyton rolled the end of her tongue again. "He's not so bad. He has a good heart."

"Where is it? In his crotch?"

She let out a little huff. Then grinned. "Yeah, pretty much." Peyton gripped the corner of the ledge and rocked forward. "I'm just saying it's normal and natural for us to do it. To want to. We're programmed for sex. It's instinct, and hormones, and drive."

"We're fucking sex machines," I deadpanned.

"Exactly." She looked at me. "You know it's true."

Heat rose up my neck. "Do you really want to do it with Chad?" I asked.

She opened her mouth, then shut it. Her shoulders slumped. "Don't tell him."

"Are you kidding me?" Peyton, I thought, raise your standards. "Chad!" I hollered toward the quad. "Get a condom —"

Peyton's hand flew at my mouth. I intercepted it with a stiff wrist. The force was unexpected and Peyton slipped off the wall, stumbling on her landing. I jumped down to catch her. Or cushion her fall. We ended up in each other's arms.

I let go fast. One of her flip-flops bounced to the wall and I retrieved it. Crouching, I helped her back into it. Flashback. We're kids playing Cinderella. It's our favorite role play. Peyton's the princess. I'm the prince. We get married in her playhouse.

It took a moment before Peyton realized I was clutching her ankle. She kicked back harder than necessary.

I staggered to stand. "Like I'd ever want you," I snarled. I recovered my books and stalked off.

"Aimee." She raced up in front of me. "I'm sorry. I didn't mean . . ." Her chin dropped. "Stupid." She shook her head. "I'm sorry. I just don't know how to act with you."

A minute passed. We stood there, avoiding each other's eyes. Wow, people grow apart. People you think you'll always be friends with. The princess turns into a frog. The prince falls on her ass.

"Is it the same for you?" Peyton asked. Her voice sounded funny. Was she scared of me? She should be. I was a dangerous dyke.

What'd she mean, the same for me? When I didn't answer

right away, she added, "When you meet a girl. Do you want to, like —"

"Fuck her?"

Peyton's eyes widened.

"I like to know her name first," I said.

She smacked my shoulder. "Seriously."

Seriously? "Yeah," I answered. "I guess it's the same. I don't know."

"But only girls?"

"And chipmunks."

She whapped me again.

"I don't want to do Chad Bennett, if that's what you're asking. Or any guy."

"Have you had sex?"

My jaw dropped.

"Sorry." She grimaced. "It's none of my business."

"No," I said. "Not yet." Don't ask me why I told her that.

"Me neither," she said.

"Seriously?"

She frowned. Her face paled. "Why? What have you heard?"

I scoffed. "Like anyone talks to me."

A clot of cheerleaders bounced by and went, "Hey, Pey."

"Hey." She waited until they passed. Biting her lip, she said, "I've come close. I haven't had intercourse." She blinked. "Do you have intercourse?"

"Only with chipmunks."

She balled a fist in my face.

I didn't know what to say. What's the equivalent? When does a lesbian lose her virginity? "I'm not sure," I admitted. "I'll let you know when I figure it out."

She smiled. She still had that one deep dimple.

Peyton said, "Can I give you a lift somewhere?" She reached into her purse and fished out her keys. "Mom actually let me have the car today."

"How is your mom?" I asked. Last I heard her parents had split too. I'd wanted to call her so bad. Reconnect.

I should've taken the step. I cared. You know? I knew how it felt.

"She's okay," Peyton answered. "She works too hard. She has a boyfriend now." Peyton rolled her eyes. "Doug."

"Duuug," I imitated her.

She stuck out her tongue stud. "They don't practice abstinence. I can hear them through the wall."

"Ew. Gross."

"Totally."

The thought of my mom ever doing it . . .

"I could drop you off at home," Peyton said. "Say hi to your mom."

"Sure. Okay. She'd like that."

We walked to the parking lot together. Out of nowhere, Peyton said, "I've missed you, Aimes. I'm glad we talked today. Why did we stop talking?"

"You tell me," I said. "You dumped me."

"No, I didn't!" She whirled. "You moved."

"We still went to the same school. You're the one who moved — away from me."

She hesitated. "You were different. You were. . . . You didn't need me anymore."

"Yes, I did! I needed you more than ever!" I was almost shouting. My parents got divorced. I was coming out. I needed her.

She pressed her tongue against her teeth. "I wanted to call you so many times."

"Why didn't you?"

"I don't know. Why didn't *you*?"

My eyes pooled with tears. She blinked real fast.

"Stupid," she muttered.

Yeah. Stupid. Abstinence is emptiness. Unnatural separation. It doesn't make sense.

Unexpectedly, Peyton hugged me. I couldn't remember the last time anyone had hugged me.

Peyton unlocked the car doors and we both got in. "Hey, Pey?" I buckled up.

She cranked over the ignition. "Yeah?"

I said, "If you're choosing between abstinence and Chad Bennett? Choose abstinence."

Boi

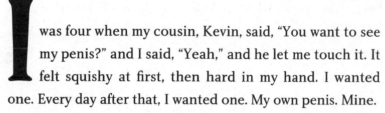

I was four when my cousin, Kevin, said, "You want to see my penis?" and I said, "Yeah," and he let me touch it. It felt squishy at first, then hard in my hand. I wanted one. Every day after that, I wanted one. My own penis. Mine.

The day I got it was the happiest day of my life. I could stop stuffing socks in my briefs. With my penis I could pack. Bind and pack. Thank you, cousin Kevin. Best bud in the world. Like a bro to me. Thank you for performing a degrading act of humiliation to buy me a penis.

I'd been binding, wrapping myself since I was twelve. Since my boobs showed through my T-shirts. Sports bras worked for a while, then my boobs got too big and I started wrapping. The best wrap was Ace Bandage. It bound real tight. I could really smash my boobs flat in stretchy wrap. Even in a sleeveless shirt, you could barely tell I was a *ze*. A s/he.

My packer was a strap-on. Guys sometimes named their penises, like Willie or Jack or Dick. Real creative. Me, I had more respect for mine. It wasn't an object; it wasn't detached or separate from me. My packer was a part of me. It made me. The shaft was big in size, six inches. Four bucks an inch. $23.99. You could get soft packers online, cock socks and compression vests. But I didn't have a credit card. You had to be twenty-one to buy at Fascinations and you had to show ID. I asked, begged, pleaded with Kevin to buy me a packer. Please, Kevin? Please? He refused to set foot in a place like that, a sex shop. I told him I'd clean his apartment for a year. I told him I'd scoop his cat box. I'd iron his boxers. I'd scour his john. Please, Kevin. PLEASE.

The day he agreed I came as close to crying as I ever had.

Kevin insisted on cash so incriminating evidence wouldn't show up on his Visa. When he hustled back to the truck and flung the paper bag at me, he said, between clenched teeth, "Don't ever ask me to do something like that again, Eva."

"Vince, not Eva," I reminded him. "I promise. Thanks." I wouldn't. I'd treasure my P. I'd guard it with my life. "Thanks, Kevin."

I could either tuck it into the harness that wound around my hips and joined at the pubic bone, or I could tape the shaft behind, between my legs. The harness straps were white elastic. Not black leather, like porn or anything. It was built for utility.

I liked the thickness of it — of me — in the mirror, standing forward, to the side, astride a chair. But for school, for public use, I'd duct tape it underneath. That way no one would know I was packing and I could feel the security of it between my legs at all times.

Oh man. Thanks, Kevin. My P was sweet.

∞

Mom dumped me on Grams and Gramps when I was a baby. That was fine. Mom was nineteen and a junkie. Who needed that? She showed up to reclaim me years later, but it was too late, you know? She'd cleaned up; got a new life, a new husband. She had a son now too. I have news for you, Mom. You got two sons. A bio boy and a trans boi.

I told Grams I didn't even want to see my mom. Ex-mom. She'd crossed my mind exactly twice in sixteen years. Once when I wondered how I got born a girl when I wasn't. Twice when I blamed her for polluting the gene pool. Kids, this is your DNA on drugs.

Grams and Gramps raised me. They raised Kevin too. We were their only grandkids. They hadn't done so well raising their own kids, my mom and uncle, who both turned out like crap. I guess by the second time around you've learned from your mistakes. You do it right.

I'd probably go live with Kevin after high school unless Grams needed me. She was getting up there. Kevin graduated two years ago and was going to trade school part-time to be a mechanic. That guy could fix anything. He was always tinkering with the toaster or a leaky faucet or a baby bird with a broken wing. When I was eight, some nasty boys busted up my bike. They stole it and slashed the tires and bent the frame. They must've rammed that bike into the side of a house a hundred times to mangle the handlebars so bad. I figured I'd be a pedestrian from then on, but there came Kevin with my bike, carting the pieces home in a wagon. He hammered at that frame in the garage all night and was still hammering away the next morning. When I got home from school there was my bike sitting in the driveway looking brand-new. It wasn't that new to begin with. That baby gleamed.

Kevin had a way with broken parts, and people. He stayed by Gramps's bedside that whole last month of the cancer. They talked sports and cars and gladiolas. Gramps loved his garden. Kevin loved working on cars, vintage models. He kept Gramps's T-bird purring like a kitten. Until the day we buried Gramps, that car hummed a happy tune. After the funeral, Kevin set it on fire and pushed it off a cliff.

∞

On Wednesday Kevin picked me up to take me to work. Right away he knew something was different. "That's a new look for you, dude," he said, checking me out as I slid into his Hummer. I buckled up.

"Yeah. Chicks were crawlin' all over me today." I straight-ened the slipknot on my tie.

Kevin snorted. He checked the rearview and popped the clutch.

Kevin got me. Grams was going blind from macular degen-eration or something so she wasn't on my case so much anymore about the crew cut. She didn't notice I'd started wearing Gramps's clothes either. Kevin noticed. He didn't yell at me or anything. Just looked me over. Approved, I guess. I didn't find myself doused with gasoline and plung-ing off a cliff.

Gramps's clothes were fine. White long-sleeved shirts with cuffs and cuff links. Long, thick ties. Tweed jackets with suede or corduroy elbow patches. Man, these were distinc-tive for their day. I had to cut off the pant legs, but I let 'em hang long and frayed. I knotted the laces on my work shoes.

People stared. Behind my back they scathed me. What else was new? I worked for many years perfecting my persona. It wasn't only the clothes Kevin picked up on. I'd always dressed like a boi. Today, I thought, it was my fresh attitude. I was authentic. Binding and packing. Wearing my P. Could everyone tell?

Kevin pulled into Fazoli's to let me out for work. "Dude, what time you get off tonight?" he asked.

"Eleven."

He checked his watch. "I might be a little late. Therèsa's coming over to study."

"Uh-huh."

"Study, dude."

"Right. I get it." I wasn't stupid. He was doing his girl. I wish I had me a girl. "I can walk home," I told him.

"No," he said. "Just wait for me. I'll call if it's going to be more than fifteen or twenty minutes."

"You're slowing down in your old age. You need a hit of Viagra?" I smirked.

He shook his head. "I mean it, Valentino."

"Vince." Stop messing with me, I shot him a glare. I changed my name a lot, but it'd been Vince all month. Not Valentino. Not Eva. Especially not Eva, the name my mother gave me. I opened the door and got out of the Hummer. "Give my love to Therèsa." I pooched my lips. Then held myself like a guy and went, "Hunh."

Kevin shook his head again, but a smile cricked his lips. "You're too much."

"For you to handle. Let me know when you set Therèsa free."

Kevin gunned the motor and backed up. I headed inside to work.

Jerome, my shift mate, was a cool bro. We'd play gangsta rap and jive each other while we piled pasta onto plates and slathered marinara over the edge. We'd make lewd jokes about the meatballs and sausage. "A squirt of juice here," Jerome'd say. "Yes, ma'am. Meaty balls." We'd arrange them with anatomical exactness on the plate. Jerome high-fived me in greeting, then hitched his chin toward the front counter. "We got us some tasty new chik-fil-ay."

"Yeah?" I swiveled my head. A new girl was training up front with Broomhilda. Right away I knew me and Jerome would be vying for this girl's attentions. She was hot.

I strung on my apron and got busy with the dinner rush. A couple of hours later, Broomhilda cranked back to the kitchen to hassle us. She was a scary bitch. Her real name was Honey Bea, if you can even imagine. The names parents give their kids. Eva. Honey Bea. When I have a kid, I'm going to name it Jesse or Mel. Something ambiguous. Free-choosing.

Honey Bea was on the eternal rag. She barked orders at us like we were deaf dogs. "Why is that tray of breadsticks out on the counter?" she woofed. "I told you they'd get hard. Who dropped the parmesan on the floor and didn't sweep up? We'll have rats in here."

Jerome muttered, "More 'n onc?"

I stifled a snort.

"Don't just stand around. Unload the dishwasher."

The other girl, the new girl, looked terrorized. Broomhilda said, "Jerome, show Nevaeh where the pasta forks go."

"I know where I'd like to stick one," he said.

Broomhilda tore his flesh with eye shrapnel. Jerome yawned and went, "I'm on my break right now, Ms. Honey. It can wait a few minutes. Anyways, I'm beat. How 'bout you, Vinnie?"

"Vince," I corrected him. "Yeah, I'm eviscerated." Everyone looked at me, like, huh? Kevin and I used to play a lot of Balderdash with Grams and Gramps. Before the cancer.

Eviscerated. Right. We'd had maybe three customers in the last twenty minutes.

Nevaeh, in particular, had glommed onto me. Shit. She heard my voice. Soon as I could, I was starting testosterone. It'd lower my voice and turn my fuzz into real facial hair. I couldn't wait for the day I could afford T.

The front door dinged and Honey Bea stormed out to assist the public. Nevaeh stayed behind, staring at me.

"Heaven spelled backward, right?" I said.

She blinked, but her eyes didn't warm.

Jerome said, "Wazzat?"

I turned to explain. "Nevaeh's name. It's heaven spelled backward. My mom was named that." She extracted my name from hers.

"Was?" Jerome said. "She dead?"

I hesitated. "Yeah." To me she was.

"Hey, I'm sorry. I didn't know." He held up a palm to high-five me. I slapped him and he gave my hand a squeeze. Stepping forward toward Nevaeh, Jerome pressed the same palm to his chest. "I'm Jerome Kahlil Monteh Nathanial Washington the third," he said. "You can call me stud nut. This here's Vinnie." His arm swept to the side to indicate me.

"Vince." Dammit. Get it right. I extended my hand. She

gazed at it for a long second, then shook it. More obliging than willing. She let go fast. She had long, elegant fingers. Fake nails all manicured and lacquered. She wouldn't be scraping the grill or chopping chicken strips anytime soon.

"I need help out front." Broomhilda's gnarly face swelled up like an ogre under the heat lamps.

Jerome answered in a lowered voice, "Lady, you need help in front, in back, in every which way."

I couldn't smother my laugh. Nevaeh said, "Are you a girl?"

Out of the blue. Just like that.

I swallowed hard.

"Sorry," she said, lowering her eyes. "I couldn't tell."

Boi, I thought. I'm boi. Transman. Born girl, but changing over. One day, soon as I get the money for T. For surgery to remove my breasts, maybe.

Honey Bea, for once, saved the day by posting the customer's order and sniping, "Nevaeh! You take this."

She startled, almost leaping onto the stove.

Jerome snatched the order off the carousel. Nevaeh squinted her eyes at Honey Bea's retreating back. She said, "Already I hate this job."

"Don't quit," I told her. "Give it a few days. Broomhilda's just testing you. Exercising her authority over you, or determining if she can."

"Yeah," Nevaeh said. "Well, she can exercise it over my gone ass."

"Ah, don't sweat it." I took a toothpick out of my pocket and rolled it between my teeth. "I'll protect you." I winked at her and balled a fist to jab her shoulder lightly. I only touched her arm playfully, but she reeled back into the trash bins, making a racket.

Geez, sorry.

"I'm not that way, okay?" She circled the bins, rolling a trash can between us.

Not that way — like, human? I shrugged. "Whatever."

Jerome sauntered past with a plate of alfredo, which he slid under the heat lamp and announced, "Order up. One snarf and barf to go."

Honey Bea scuttled over and scowled at him. Some people have no sense of humor.

There was a queue of customers around eight-thirty, nine, then it died again. Me and Jerome busied ourselves in the kitchen rapping about music and chicks and politics in the Middle East. His cousin was touring Baghdad. My shift ended and I told him, "Later, man." He closed up.

"See ya, Vince." He saluted. "Mañana."

Outside the front door, I waited for Kevin. It was a brisk night. Bracing, Gramps would say. Invigorating. "'Tis an evenin' for the Willoughbys," he'd say. I had no idea who the Willoughbys were. I should've asked when I had the chance. My breath streamed out in a vapor trail. Blow out. Suck in. I jammed my hands into Gramps's suit coat and felt my box of round toothpicks. I fingered one out and stuck it in the side of my mouth. I counted cars in the lot. Three to be exact. Not exceedingly busy at this late hour. Where was Kevin?

I leaned against the smooth brick and squeezed my thighs together to ensure it was still with me. It was.

I loved the sense of it. The sensuality. It made me feel confident and complete.

The door swung open and Nevaeh stepped out. I pushed off the wall. "Hey."

She lurched backward.

My hands came out of my pockets and I held them up. "Don't worry. I'm not contagious." I slid my hands back into the pockets, balling my fists hard against my thighs.

Her breath willowed up and dispersed in a mist. Her eyes swept the parking lot and she shivered.

My first instinct was to offer her my jacket, but wow. She was cold to me. "You waitin' for someone?" I asked. Her boyfriend, probably.

She nodded. "My brother."

What, no boyfriend? She had to have a boyfriend. Hot girl like her?

I couldn't take my eyes off her. She was . . . I forced myself to glance away. Out of bounds.

"Look, I didn't mean anything, okay? I'm just not that way."

I twisted my head back slowly. "Yeah, I get it. I wasn't coming on to you." Much.

Our eyes held. Hers broke off first. She gazed into the

distance and murmured, "He's always late. I can't stand when people are late. It's so rude." She scuffed the sidewalk with her boot.

"I know. I hate it too. I'm always on time."

"Me too. I'm, like, anal about it."

I grinned. We had that in common. I took the extended conversation as a truce.

"How long have you been working here?" she asked.

"Me?" I said. " 'Bout eight months."

"Wow."

I'm steady, I wanted to say. Reliable.

"I worked at Kmart for almost a year before they shut the store," she said.

"The one in Four Points?"

"Yeah."

"I shopped there all the time," I said.

She hugged herself. "You're the only one."

"I need —" "I want —" we both began at once. And cracked up.

"Go ahead," I told her.

"I need to work," she said, "so I can pay for my dance lessons."

"You're a dancer?" I tried not to check out her body, but my eyes had a mind of their own. "You look it," I said.

Her eyes fell. "Thanks." Rubbing her hands together, she added, "I'm not going to stand here all night." Nevaeh pivoted and hurried down the sidewalk in the direction of the drive-up window.

"Hey." I hustled to catch up. "You shouldn't be out walking alone. Not in this neighborhood." Impulsively, I reached over to touch her. She flinched. I withdrew my hand quick. "It's dark. The streetlights are all shot out. Can I walk you home?"

"No!" Her voice softened. "But thanks."

A car squealed around the corner and flooded us in headlights. Tires crunched gravel and the fender overshot the curb. Instinct made me pull Nevaeh back a foot. Two guys hauled out of the car and swaggered up to us. "Nev, you okay?" One of them clenched Nevaeh's upper arm and jerked her away from me. "This guy bothering you?" he said.

The other dude, the taller one with a dirty cut on his cheek, checked me out.

"Yes," Nevaeh answered.

What? I think she meant, Yes, she was okay, but the guy misinterpreted. Both dudes did. They were on me before I knew what was happening.

My heel hit the edge of sidewalk and the sticker bush behind me poked into my back. "Hey, it's cool." Both guys had a grip on my arms. "I wasn't doing anything. I didn't touch her."

"Eric, come on," Nevaeh said. "Leave her alone. Let's go."

I assumed Eric was her brother. He positioned me in front

of him, straight on. "Her? Did you say 'her'?" His eyes stripped me down. They paused at my chest.

"Fuck," the other dude said. "Are you a girl?" His lip curled, wrinkling the cut, making it more ominous. Hoisting his hands onto his hips, surveying me like a specimen, he added, "You one of them freaks? A crosser? A transvestite?"

"Everything's cool," I said. My voice held firm. I'm not a transvestite. The sticker bush began to prickle through Gramps's pants.

Someone in the car hollered, "What's up?"

Cut-face replied, "Moby. Come check out this freak." He reached forward and twisted the sleeve of my jacket, pulling me toward him. A car door slammed.

"He's a she. A she-he."

Ze, I thought.

"No way," the third guy said. Moby was bigger than the first two, a giant. Like two ninety.

"There's only one way to be sure," Nevaeh's brother said. He grinned at Cut-face, then me.

"Man, hey, it's cool." I wriggled out of Cut-face's clutches. And Eric's. My pulse raced. I fought down the fear. I knew if I let them see fear . . .

Two of them lunged at me, trapping my arms behind my back. They reeked of beer and weed and cigarettes.

A sudden chill on my stomach made me gasp. They'd lifted up my shirt. "Oh shit. Look at that."

All three gawked. Eric or Moby, one of them, put his

face up to mine and said, "What's the matter, sweetcakes? You shy?"

"Eric, stop." Nevaeh's voice, small and far away. "You guys."

His hand scraped down the front of my wrap and yanked forward. The Ace Bandage budged maybe an inch. It held firm. His forehead touched my breastbone and he said, "There's something down there." His hands pressed against both my breasts. "Oh yeah. I see cleavage." He inserted an index finger between me.

"Cut it out." I pushed him off. I kicked him and missed. "Pervert."

He laughed. The other two howled with laughter.

From behind, Cut-face jerked my suit coat roughly over my shoulders and down my arms. Eric got my shirt unbuttoned and the other, Moby, tore it off. Cut-face found the end of the bandage and spun me around and around as he unwrapped it. I tried to plant my feet, slap them off, kick, elbow, resist, whatever I could do, but they just kept spinning and spinning me. The wrap came free.

"Whoa," one said. "Nice rack."

Another went, "Why would you want to cover up these pretty things?"

Rough hands. Squeezing me.

A car door shut. Nevaeh? Where are you?

Someone pinched my nipple. I cried out. No, I thought. It isn't me. They're not my breasts. They're coming off. I can't feel this. I'm cool.

Cut-face tried to kiss me, but I twisted away. Animal. Moby said, "Gross, dude. You know you're kissing a guy."

"Oh yeah?" He grabbed my boobs and squeezed hard. He suctioned his lips onto mine.

A wave of nausea swam up from my stomach and I gagged. I almost hurled in Cut-face's mouth.

A hand slid between my legs. "Whoa, ho. What have we here?"

I kicked out hard, but both my wrists were clenched in vise grips. Whoever had me was strong. He bent my arms around my back. My shoulder cracked and I bit my lip to suppress a scream.

"Check. It. Out." Cut-face unzipped my pants.

Please, I prayed. Please. Nevaeh. Anyone. Someone come to Fazoli's to eat. Somebody come to the drive-up. One person, one person in this whole wide world, get hungry and want Italian.

Cold. Biting cold on my legs. Teeth?

Nevaeh's voice, "What are you doing to her?"

Eric shouting, "Nevaeh, stay out of this."

Don't, Nevaeh. Don't listen.

Eric looking at me. Making a decision. "Let's go." Stepping away.

"What?" Moby's voice. "We're just having a little fun here. You're the one who said you're bored with female shit. You're the one who wanted to go cruising and find us a cheap ho. Man, you got your wish."

Cut-face said, "Careful what you wish for." Nasty laugh.

I tried to move, run, but my pants were around my ankles.

Moby gasped. "What in the world . . . ? Hey, ho. Rubber dickie."

"Please." My voice trembled. Please, God, I prayed into the sky. Gramps, if you're up there.

The duct tape ripped and a hunk of pubic hair came with it. I cried out. I couldn't help it. "She's bigger than you, Moby." Cut-face laughed.

Someone screamed. Was that me? Roaring, humming in my ears.

Pressure, pulling on it. Yanking. Then the elastic snapping off my hips.

A horn honked and the sticker bush scraped my legs. My face met concrete. A shoe on my head.

"Hey!" Kevin's voice. "Hey!" Louder.

Running.

Kevin kneeling next to me. "Eva?" His arms snaking around me, pulling me up into his chest. The smell of Therèsa's sweet perfume.

"Did they hurt you?" His face in my face. A car squealing away.

I couldn't move. Couldn't answer. Consciousness swam to the surface, barely. Oxygenation. Breathe. Inhalate. Is that a word, Gramps? "Give her back," I said. My voice sounded hollow, detached.

Kevin bent his head. "What?"

Conviction now. "Give her back!" On solid ground. What is this? Wet? My cheeks, my eyes.

Kevin's arms flexed around me and gathered me in. "Oh, Eva."

No. Sobbing, hiccuping. "Vince," I spat at him. Why can't he remember? "It's —"

"Vince," he said. "I got it."

"It's mine," I told him, swiping my eyes, my nose. "I want it back."

Kevin held my head against his chest. "Never mind." I felt his cheek brush my crew, back and forth. "Never mind," he said again. "Whatever it is, I'll fix it."

No, I thought, you can't fix this. "I've been waiting so long." It came out a wail. Was that my voice? "I saved up the money. I made you buy it." Humiliation. Degradation.

"Forget it, Vince." He held me another minute. I was crying so hard I couldn't talk. I was gulping in breaths, and choking. Kevin finally loosened his grip and retrieved Gramps's suit coat, which was stuck in the holly bush behind us, and wrapped me up in it.

I still felt naked.

"I'll get you a new one. The next one's on me," Kevin said. "You can get a bigger one — my size." He grinned. "Don't worry, Vince." He looked at me deep. "I'll replace it."

"You can't."

"I will."

"You *can't!*" Didn't he get it? He couldn't replace it. He couldn't fix this.

"Never mind. You'll be okay."

I'll never be okay. What they took, what they stole from me, it's damage. Damage beyond repair.

TIAD

Scar_tissu: My gf dumped me 2day. Someone. Pleeez. Tell me how 2 deal. I lv her so much. I want 2 end it. I want 2 die. Anybody out there? HELP ME.

Black_Venus: Scar_tissu, STOP. I'm here. Don't do anything rash. Listen to me. It'll get better. One day at a time. I can't know how you feel, but when my gf told me she didn't love me anymore, I thought my life was over. I walked around like a zombie for weeks. I cried so hard my eyes swelled shut. You're not alone. We're here for you. You're going to make it, OK? You're going to heal. I promise. Give it time.

Sunshlne26: I'm so sorry this happened 2 U. I'm here for U 2. We all R. Tlk 2 us.

Bikrchik: scar, u don't no me. but maybe if u talk about wt happened, u'll feel better. wat did she say xactly?

Scar_tissu: I can't repeat it. I don't want 2 remember. I want 2 die.

Black_Venus: NO. You don't. She's not worth it. No one is worth you dying for. Do you hear me?

Bikrchik: i been where u r

Sunshine26: Me 2

Black_Venus: Scar_tissu, we know your heart is aching. The pain and longing and loneliness are unbearable. It hurts so bad.

Scar_tissu: Yeh. My stomach feels like someone stabbed me. I can't eat. I can't sleep. I'm bleeding 2 death.

Black_Venus: You are going to get through this. I swear. I'll stay here all night if you need me. I can tell you're a really sensitive person and that you loved your gf deeply. That's what makes love so good, and so bad.

Scar_tissu: I lv'd her with all my heart. I still do. I never lv'd anyone like that. I wantd to be with her 4ever. I asked her to marry me.

Sunshine26: Maybe that scared her. Maybe she wasn't ready.

Scar_tissu: She said yes. She wanted the same thing. We made plans for when we turned 18 and everythng. After grad, we were going to find an apartmnt. Then I found out she was

Bikrchik: POP GG

Scar_tissu: What's that? I'm sorry, I hvn't been on the board b4. What's POP? What's GG?

Black_Venus: Parents on Patrol. Gotta Go. You found out she was what?

Scar_tissu: Cheating

Sunshine26: Oh, Scar. Oh no. I'm so sorry.

Black_Venus: Me too. You didn't deserve that kind of treatment. Your gf betrayed your trust. She isn't worthy of your love.

Scar_tissu: But I lv her so much.

Bikrchik: i'm bck. sorree. evil rent

Scar_tissu: I can't liv w/o her. I want her back.

Black_Venus: No you don't. She'll do it to you again.

Bikrchik: do wat?

Sunshine26: Black_Venus's right. She isn't worth it. U can't trust her

Bikrchik: wat she do xactly? wat I miss?

Sunshine26: Her gf cheated on her.

Bikrchik: fk hr. i hate grls who play

Sunshine26: You have to move on, Scar.

Scar_tissu: It isn't that easy. There aren't any grls here where I liv. She's the only 1.

Black_Venus: Your love is pure. But if you got her back, would you ever be able to look at her the same way? Love her as much?

Sunshine26: Good question.

Gypsygrl: Hi grlfrnds. Wat, or who, r we chattng about?

A pop-up message blinked on my screen. Mail. I had e-mail. Should I read it? It could be from Dylan. But I was in the middle of chat. What if it was Dylan? I risked it.

Scar_tissu,

Hi. It's me, Black_Venus. The board is getting too crowded and I wanted to talk to you alone. You need some private time. Are you there? Want to IM?

Yeh, I replied. *Thanx.*

Wow, Black_Venus wanted to talk to me. She was amazing. I'd been lurking on the chat board for a while, afraid to speak up. Until now I never had anything to say. So many people in pain over breakups and stuff. God, I never thought I'd be one of them. I switched to IM.

Black_Venus: What are you thinking? That's a stupid question. You're sad. You hurt.

Scar_tissu: Yeh. I can't stop crying.

Black_Venus: I know. You feel lost. Scared. Everything seems hopeless.

Scar_tissu: Yeh

Black_Venus: I wish I could talk to you in person. WDUL? I'm in LA.

Should I tell her? I guess it wouldn't hurt. She'd told me. She was a regular board member, so it must not be against the rules or anything.

Scar_tissu: Mason City

Black_Venus: Where's that?

Scar_tissu: IA

Black_Venus: Iowa? As in corn country?

Scar_tissu: Yeh. Hicksville. Hog farms and turkey trots.

Black_Venus: *Grins* It has to be really hard to hook up with girlz in a small town. The only thing I know about IA is corn.

Scar_tissu: Right. Corn fritters, corn dogs, corn on the cob. Everyone is corn fed.

Black_Venus: LOL. I think I flew over IA once on my way to Boston.

Scar_tissu: That was me in the cornfield below screaming, "Stop! Emergency landing. Take me with U."

Black_Venus: LMAO. I must've had my earbuds in. I'm glad to see you're smiling. Feeling better?

Scar_tissu: Yeh. Thanx. It still hurts.

Black_Venus: I know. You're going to hurt for a while. Give yourself time. Just keep telling yourself TIAD.

TIAD. What was that?

Black_Venus: Tomorrow Is Another Day.

Right. Another day without her, I thought.

Black_Venus: Can we IM later tonight too? I think you're cool. I'd like to get to know you better.

My pulse raced. She thought I was cool. Black_Venus thought I was cool. A girl from LA? Wow.

Black_Venus: What do you listen to? What's on your playlist?

She'd think it was stupid. I could lie. No, that was no way to start a relationship. A relationship? What was I saying? We weren't in a relationship.

Scar_tissu: Tera Moses. Mostly. But I like all kinds of music.

Black_Venus: Tera Moses?!!! OMG. I love them. No one else I know appreciates their sound.

Yeah. No one I knew did either. Dylan couldn't stand them. Black_Venus and I had a connection.

Black_Venus: Who else do you like?

Scar_tissu: Limping Fetus. Pink. Archimedes. EZ Girl.

Black_Venus: OMG. We're so in sync. Do you like Melia?

Scar_tissu: Yeh. I love her! She's awesome. Did you see her video of "Blown Away"?

Black_Venus: Sexy, huh? Plus, I know her personally. She went to my school for a year.

Scar_tissu: Melia? Wow. Is that her real name? What's she like in person?

Black_Venus: Kind of a bitch. But . . . pant pant, I could get beyond her putrid personality. Her real name is Amelia Corncob. Not really. It's Amelia Trottenturkey.

I laughed.

We IM'd more about music, movies. She was into the scene, the Hollywood scene, West Coast scene. I wasn't sure how old she was, but older than me. We talked until Dad told me to shut it down and go to bed.

∞

Her ID on my screen every morning was my only reason to get up. Black_Venus. I wondered what it meant. When I chose Scar_tissu, I had no idea it would predict my future. We IM'd for a week, every day. We'd chat for, like, an hour in the morning, then I'd have to tear off to school to make first period. Classes dragged. I didn't have a cell phone and we couldn't use the computers at school for e-mail. When the last bell rang I was out of there, racing home to hook up with Black_ Venus. She always seemed to be waiting.

Black_Venus: What'd you do today?

Scar_tissu: Slept. Zoned. What'd U do?

Black_Venus: Shopped. I'm addicted. Did you see her today?

My throat caught.

Me: No. She's avoiding me.

Black_Venus: Gee, I can't imagine why. How are you doing?

Me: Better.

A little. A few pangs of loneliness and despair, but I wasn't feeling as hopeless or . . . used. Bruised on the inside. How could I not have known? Dylan canceling out on me. Having other plans every Friday night. Her tone of voice, weird vibes. Her distraction while we kissed. Her lack of enthusiasm. Me, finding out from friends about her other girl in Lincoln. God, that was the worst. Then giving Dylan the ultimatum: Choose. "Choose, Dylan."

She did. Now I was more angry at myself for being stupid.

Black_Venus: I know what you're thinking. How could you not have known? I'll tell you how. You were in love. It's easy to fool people when they don't want to see.

Or hear. I never want to hear those words again: "I don't choose you."

Me: Thanx. I needed 2 hear that.

It wouldn't happen to me again. Ever. Live and learn.

∞

Black_Venus: What's your idea of a romantic evening? And BTW, I refuse to call you Scar_tissu. Do you have another screen name? Or a real name?

I considered telling her. We'd always been honest. . . .

Me: Hayley

Black_Venus: Hayley. Yeah, it fits you. Sweet name.

Me: It was my mom's favorite name. She died when I was a baby.

Long pause.

Black_Venus: I'm sorry. So much pain in your life.

Me: Like I said, I was a baby. I never knew her.

Black_Venus: Sometimes that's a blessing. Mothers can be . . . you know. So, Hayley. What do you look like? The pic you posted on the board is a fairy. Did you draw that?

Me: Yeh

I loved fairies. Ever since I was little, I'd been captivated by them. No wonder — I was one. Ha ha. I wished I could fly away or disappear in fairy dust.

How to describe myself?

Me: I'm ordinary. Brwn hair. Brwn eyes.

Black_Venus: You're not ordinary. I bet you're beautiful.

Dad said I was pretty, but he was biased.

Black_Venus: Post a pic of yourself on the board.

No way. That'd be the end of this relationship. Anyway, I didn't have a picture I liked. She was gorgeous. Her photo was slick, like a professional studio shot. Black and white. Airbrushed.

Black_Venus: OK, Hayley. COS: Change of Subj. Romantic evening. I'd suddenly appear outside your door in my silver XL. The cornstalks would be waving in the wind.

Me: LOL. Really.

Black_Venus: I'm wearing a black bodysuit with a vamp cape. I bow to you, kiss your hand, and take a nibble.

Wow, she was getting into this. Like a role play. I couldn't. . . . Yes, I could. Why not?

Me: Mmm. How do I taste?

Black_Venus: Salty. But you're sea salt. Natural and pure. I may have to fill a shaker for later.

Me: Not too much later. I'm ready now.

I blushed. I couldn't believe I typed that.

Black_Venus: I draw back the cape and whip out a box of imported French chocolates. Truffles.

Me: Ah oui. How did you know I love ze chocolat?

Black_Venus: When I think of you, when I close my eyes at night and imagine you, you're dressed in a cornflower blue silk negligee I saw at Victoria's Secret on Saturday. I thought, Oh yeah. Iowa. Shuck it off and get in my car.

Me: LMAO. UMMH.

Someone used that on the board once: U Make Me Hot.

Black_Venus: It's all good. What are you wearing right now?

What was I wearing? My uniform from school. Navy skirt and white blouse. That wouldn't play in Hollywood.

Me: Nothing

Black_Venus: *Squeals*

Me: I lied. I'm wearing a wet T-shirt. With no bra.

Black_Venus: Heavy breathing. In the car (which is a convertible, BTW), we lower the seats and spread out. Oops, did I say spread? I open a bottle of champagne and pour you a flute. (I happen to keep 2 champagne flutes in the glove box at all times.)

Me: Who doesn't?

Black_Venus: *Grins* We eye each other through the champagne bubbles. I say, "Hayley, what should we toast to?"

Me: Love

No response. I waited.

I'd said something wrong. I'd scared her off. It was too much, too soon. Love? What was I thinking? We were just kidding around. Playing a game. Making sexual innuendos. Not serious.

Me: Or lust

I wished I could take back love. Delete, delete, delete. Still no answer.

Me: Are you there?

Black_Venus: Let me ask you something, Hayley. Are you ready for love?

Was I?

Black_Venus: Because . . . to tell you the truth . . . I know it's really fast but . . . you're the nicest person I've ever met and . . . I feel this deep connection with you and . . . oh, what the hell. I could fall in love with you.

My heart leapt out of my chest. Did she mean it?

Black_Venus: You wouldn't know what hit you.

∽

I lay in bed, curled on my side, staring at my computer. Two weeks and two days had passed since my heart had been shattered, my world blown apart. "I don't choose you, Hayley." Dylan, how cruel. Even though the words still stung, the ache had dulled. My heart was mending. It seemed longer ago, like a horrible accident that happened in the past to another person. A car crash. The only victim is bleeding profusely and rushed to the ER for immediate medical attention. She's put on life support. The life support brings her back from the dead, practically. Her open wounds close and heal, the scars become almost indistinguishable. Scar tissue dissolves. Thanks to Black_Venus. Thanks to new love. I never thought I'd love again. I never thought I could.

I was lying in the same position when my eyes opened the next morning. My hands were pressed together under my cheek. The computer beckoned.

I got up and logged on.

Me: Black_Venus, are U there?

Black_Venus: Yes, Hayley. I'm here. I'll always be here.

Me: What you said. About loving me? I feel the same.

There was an interlude. The stark contrast between light and dark. Sent, received.

Black_Venus: Say it. Tell me how you feel.

Me: I'm in love with you.

Black_Venus: I mean, I need to hear you say it out loud. Can I call you?

∞

The LDR was official. Once I heard her voice, the connection between us was physical. It wasn't anything like the long-distance relationships I'd heard or read about. I know everybody says you can't have a relationship with a person long-distance, but what do they know? Have they tried? You can. You can determine a lot by how a person sounds on the phone, by what she says, how she says it. Her voice, her laugh. Your voices fill each other's heads. You can tell.

Ceylon, that was her real name. Ceylon. How cool. She had this Spice Island voice. Curry and cloves. Middle Eastern maybe, or Indian. She did look exotic in her picture.

"You're laughing more," Ceylon said. "You have a beautiful laugh."

I blushed. "So do you."

"You can tell so much by a person's laughter. The kindness of her heart. The generosity of her soul. You are a giving, loving person, Hayley."

I never knew how to respond to flattery. I should compliment her back. Dad tapped on my door. "Kiddo, I'm turning in."

"Okay," I called. "Sleep tight."

Ceylon said, "Why don't you come to bed — with me?"

A laugh lodged in my throat.

"I'm already in bed," she said. "Lying here naked. Take off your clothes and lie with me."

My breath caught. "Okay. Hang on." I waited until I heard Dad's door click. Stripping, I slid under the sheets. I clamped the phone to my ear. "I'm here."

"I can feel how beautiful you are, Hayley," Ceylon said. "Inside and out."

"Thanks. I mean, you too." This was happening. It was.

"Are you with me?" she said.

"I am."

We lay together, breathing, connecting. After a minute, I asked the question. "When can we meet?"

Ceylon didn't answer.

"Did you hear me?"

"Shh."

"When is your spring break?" I asked. "Mine's in two weeks."

She said, "I'd have to look."

A tingle of excitement under my skin. What if we could really be together?

She added, "But my family always goes to Majorca that week."

Majorca? Where was that?

"It's off the coast of Spain." She read my mind again.

Spain. Wow.

"Where do you go on spring break?"

I clicked my tongue. "Dubuque. It's a lot like Spain, minus the Spaniards."

"And the beaches, the paella, the bikini babes." She laughed.

Bikini babes?

"Just kidding." Ceylon laughed again. She had a heady laugh. Low and husky. "Even though you're far away, I feel you in my heart. I sleep with you; dream with you."

I wouldn't mind sleeping with her — minus the sleep.

"Any possibility you can fly out here some weekend?" I asked.

She didn't answer.

"Or I could come to you." Yeah, right. That was going to happen. Ceylon owned that fully equipped silver XL convertible and really did shop in downtown LA. We owned a broken-down '63 Plymouth and I shopped at Target.

"Do you mind if I ask how old you are?" I said. Not that it mattered. It didn't matter if I liked older women. Dylan was a senior. Forget Dylan.

Ceylon said, "Seventeen."

That's all? She seemed . . .

"Let me guess," Ceylon said. "You're . . . fifteen?"

"Sixteen," I corrected.

"Damn. I'm usually good at guessing. I hope I didn't insult you."

"No. Not at all." What'd she mean "usually"?

"Carol just came in," Ceylon said. "GG."

"IM me later," I blurted as she hung up. To myself, in the dark, I added in a whisper, "I love you."

Carol was her mother. Ceylon called her mother by her first name. How cool is that?

∞

Black_Venus: I wrote a poem for you.

Me: For me or for your beach babes?

Long pause.

Black_Venus: Don't be like that. I haven't given you any reason to be jealous.

My face flared. I couldn't help it. I didn't want her to leave for a week.

Black_Venus: Do you want to hear it?

Me: Yeh, of course. I'm sorry. I love U.

Black_Venus: Here goes:

Curious mosaic

Continental drift

Parabolic metaphor

Elemental rift

Time and transposition

Conscious intermission

Assertion?

Desertion —

Black_Venus: That's all I have so far. You finish it.

Me: How about "Spanish Inquisition."

Black_Venus: I don't get it.

Neither did I. It rhymed. I didn't understand one word of that poem.

Black_Venus: How about, Esteem her/Redeem her. Something something lift.

Me: Okay. Good.

That really cleared it up — not.

Black_Venus: Can I ask you a personal question, Hayley?

Me: Yeh

Black_Venus: Are you a virgin?

My stomach clenched. Should I tell her the truth?

Black_Venus: Sorry, didn't mean to pry. That's out of line.

Me: No. No. I'm just wondering how many beach babes I'd be compared with.

She signed off.

∞

I thought I'd die of loneliness while she was in Spain. I researched Majorca on MapQuest and calculated the distance from Mason City to the coast of Spain. 81,000,000 miles, I think. That might've been air miles, or kilometers, or dots on the legend. I'm not too good with maps. Halfway around the world, anyway. No distance at all if she'd IM. Or call. We spoke before she left and she assured me I had NOTHING TO WORRY ABOUT. I should think about myself, she said. She said she probably wouldn't have Internet access in the villa they were renting. She said I should finish the poem. I said, "Send it to me on a postcard."

All I could think about was how she was lying on the beach in a string bikini attracting babes. Beach babes. I hated Iowa. I hated being stuck here in Corncob, America, with no money or opportunity or beach babes.

Ceylon would be back Sunday. She said Sunday, I know she did. I'd been ticking off the days on my calendar. Thursday, Friday, Saturday. Starting at six thirty Sunday morning, I logged on and IM'd her.

No answer. I stowed the phone in my room in case she called. If I had to go to the bathroom, I'd string the cord as far as it would go. I'd have called her, but she never gave me her number. She wanted to, she said. She had a private number and all the free minutes she could use because her uncle was CEO of a wireless company. She didn't say which one.

Then she'd change the subject and I'd never get her number.

By nine a.m., I hadn't heard from her. Nine a.m. in Iowa is seven a.m. in LA. She might have been catching up on sleep.

Seven, eight, nine. I IM'd her over and over.

Then it was noon LA time, two o'clock Iowa. No response.

When I hadn't heard from her by seven p.m., I got frantic. I IM'd: R U there? U there? Ceylon. Are. You. There?

Monday morning, a blank screen. My eyes burned from staring at the monitor all night. Dad called up to me, "Hayley, school. Get the lead out."

I slogged to my door. "I feel sick today. Can I stay home?"

Dad appeared at the bottom of the stairs. He gazed up at me, studying my face. I know I looked like a corpse with my straggled hair and bloodshot eyes. Dad set his slice of toast on the TV and jogged up the stairs. He felt my forehead. I had to be terminally ill before he'd let me miss school. "Hang on." He hustled back downstairs.

I curled on my side on the bed. Dad returned with the thermometer. "Open." He stuck it under my tongue. We stared at each other until the thermometer beeped.

He checked it. "Sorry, kid." Dad patted my shoulder. "Normal."

Whatever that was.

At school I kept ducking into the media center, logging on to the computers to check my e-mail illegally, to IM her. Maybe her server was down. That happens, right? Wasn't MSN the server? MSN worked for me.

At lunch I called home to see if she'd left a message on the machine. There was one call from George Finkel, Dad's poker buddy, about a venue change for the game Saturday night. I hung up. My stomach plunged. What if her plane crashed? That happens. We'd never hear about it in Iowa.

There was a TV in the media center, so I switched it on. Soaps, talk shows, infomercials. It was the middle of the day. You'd think there'd be news. ABC? CNN? We didn't have cable at school. Finally, Fox News. Same old thing: weather, war, murder.

I snuck out and raced home. If I got marked truant, so what?

No mail. No postcards from Spain. One spam alert in my e-mail box. All I could think to do was log on to the chat board.

Scar_tissu: Has anyone heard from Black_Venus?

Sunshine26: Hi, Scar. How R U? I thought U were gone for good. I hoped U were.

What did that mean? She hoped I was dead?

Bikrchik: bak so soon? wat u do? fk up again?

Sunshine26: Tht's not funny. What happened, Scar? She said you were ready to love.

Who?

Scar_tissu: Black_Venus? Have U heard from her? Is she back from Spain?

There was a long silence. Then —

Bikrchik: th rain in spain

Sunshine26: She said U were saved. U didn't need us anymore.

Bikrchik: add 1 to her scorecard

Sunshine26: That's not fair. She's here to help. U know that.

Bikrchik: our savior

Willowwind: Hi, I'm new here.

Bikrchik: hey, sup, willo?

grl2grl

Willowwind: My gf broke up with me

Bikrchik: epidemik

Sunshine26: Be quiet, bikr.

Saving_grace: Hi, Willowwind. Welcome to the board. What happened with your gf?

Willowwind: She said she wasn't really "that way." She thought she was bi, but after she tried it with me, she decided she wasn't into girls.

Bikrchik: ow. bitch

Sunshine26: Bikr. God. U R really insensitive sometimes.

Bikrchik: shut up

Sunshine26: Grace, make her leave.

Saving_grace: Could we be more respectful, please? People are hurting. Willowwind, the same thing happened to me. I can't know how you feel exactly, but I wanted to die when I lost my gf. Sometimes it helps to talk about it. We're out here. We're listening. TIAD.

Two-Part Invention

When I hit the summit of Red Mountain Pass, I had to pull over to the side of the road and hurl. Never, in all my years of performing, had I suffered one anxiety attack, one wave of nausea, one skipped or hurried heartbeat. Ever since I'd made my decision to come to camp, major stomach eruption.

I cleaned myself up, wishing I had a Coke or something to swish out my mouth. My throat was raw. I hiked down to a ledge overlooking Wild Horse Canyon and gazed across the riverscape. Breathtaking view. I'd forgotten how beautiful it was up here. Remote. Sweeping. How freeing, exhilarating, to play my music in the mountains. With Annika.

Wherever I played, though, my music transcended time and space. At home in my bedroom, in a stuffy practice room at school, in a closet, garage, backstage. It wasn't my music making me sick. It was the thought of losing it.

A long lenticular cloud sluiced across the sky. Was it last year we lay on the river rocks after morning practice conjuring shapes and stories in the clouds? The ripple of water over stones filled the quiet moments. *Was* it last year? Or the year before? Hard to remember; all the summers jumbled together. Annika had said, "When I'm reincarnated, I want to return as water."

I'd laughed.

"What?" She'd angled her head up at me. "You don't think I'm worthy of water?"

"Of course you're worthy. You're a drip." It must've been last year because her hair had grown out and she was wearing it natural. "I'm just not sure I believe in reincarnation."

Annika had rolled over and propped herself on an elbow. "Really? Why not?"

"I'm not religious."

"It's not about religion." She'd plucked a blade of grass and nibbled on the tip. "Is it?"

I'd focused on her face. Her skin, so warm and brown.

"I think it is. The afterlife. Belief, faith. I guess I'm more about making my life on Earth count. Not letting it elude me."

"You mean using your gift." Annika had nudged me with her foot, and we'd laughed. Our so-called "gifts." Everyone always referred to our "God-given talents." I didn't believe in such a thing. Sure, we might be born with a natural talent, an enhanced ability for . . . something. In our cases, music. But unless you worked to develop your ability, unless you worked your ass off, all your talent did was trickle downstream and empty into the vast unknown of human potential.

Wow, that was deep for me. I'd have to tell Annika that one. No, she might tell Bryce.

Up here you could be the next Sarah Chang, the next Yo-Yo Ma — like Bryce thought he was — and still, talent alone wouldn't carry you. If you didn't practice, didn't reach, didn't maintain your level of commitment, if you had an overblown sense of yourself the way Bryce did . . .

Why was I thinking about him? He made me sick. Annika had mentioned him, again, in her last e-mail. "Bryce got a new teacher. He sez 'Fear Me Now.'"

Fear *her*, Bryce. Annika had beat him out for principal cello last year. He was stunned. I loved it.

He so obviously had the hots for her.

My stomach churned. I hauled myself up and dusted off my rear, inhaled the view one last time, and clambered up the hill to the car. I checked to make sure my case was in the front seat. Stupid to leave it out in the open with the door unlocked. Stupid to leave the car. Last thing Mom said before I tossed my duffel into the backseat was, "Don't stop for anything, Kat. Drive straight through. You don't know what kinds of crazies live up in the mountains."

Right, Mom. Cannibals and yetis. She was paranoid.

"Don't walk home alone in the dark." "Don't stay in the practice room after six." "Don't take shortcuts." "Don't talk to strangers."

Strangers. The only person in the world who didn't feel like a stranger to me was Annika.

The last stretch of road was hairpin turns. No cars on Red Mountain Pass. What if I got dizzy from altitude sickness and swerved over a cliff? The gas gauge wiggled on E. How much farther to the junction? I might be thumbing a ride the last twenty miles. Twenty miles to Annika. Twenty miles to doom.

Stop it. Stop thinking. I needed distraction.

Stravinsky's *Violin Concerto*. Saint-Saëns's *Havanaise*. All the pieces we'd be performing this summer. I should run through the passacaglia in my head, or my Paganini *Caprice* again. I was so happy to read in the program that I'd be doing the *Caprice in A Minor*. Solo violin. Even more stoked to see Martinů's *Duo #2 for Violin and Cello*. Last year Annika and I had slipped out the first night after curfew. We'd grabbed our flashlights and snuck deep into the woods to a small clearing. She'd set up her cello and perched on a low branch to balance, while I stood beneath the canopy of blue spruce. Intoxicating smell. The smell of her.

L'Air du Temps. That was the perfume Annika wore. I wonder if Bryce knew that.

We played. First Bach, to warm up. *Two-Part Inventions*. Then my two-part invention, a speed metal piece that would sound awesome on acoustic strings and synthesizer. We did the Martinů. We were lost in the dissonance, resolution, tempo changes, meter, mood, dominant/submissive. We played as one — one instrument, one voice.

There were plenty of professional string quartets, but not many duos. Annika and I both liked classical, but we loved jazz and rock and alternative and rap and even new country. We clicked. From that first year, we'd just connected. I'd been writing music for the two of us.

The two of us. Would there be a two of us? My gut twisted. Chill, Kat. It'll be fine. It'll be a medical miracle if you don't have an ulcer.

I couldn't believe this was our eighth year at St. Ives. Couldn't believe we were going to be seniors in high school. I couldn't believe I hadn't told Annika.

At the last minute I decided not to pack her cards and e-mails. I'd printed them off, of course, all her letters. Read them over and over, trying to glean a hint of anything. Beyond friendship, I mean. Any emotional tenor in her words.

Her face materialized behind my eyes and I felt myself being swept into my newest composition. It was a duet, of course, a slow, romantic piece. Long, lusty bows and sexy riffs. I called it *Strings Attached*. Why? Would there be strings attached? The refrain had emptied over and over in my sleep, my deepest REM. In my dream I'm coming in late. Always late. Coming in after the downbeat. I miss my cue and it's frustrating. I'm concentrating so hard on getting it right, getting in, once I'm in, I'm solid. I nail it. On her cello, Annika is my alter ego, my reflective voice. We play the notes by heart, of course. By soul. We master dynamics and form. This is how my most personal composition will be played. Perfect. In concert with Annika. My violin gives me presence and purpose. My music is my truth.

Annika got me. She got it. I thought I kept a killer schedule, getting up at five and practicing until school started at eight, then rushing home to put in another three or four hours before homework, finally drifting off around midnight, my fingers still buzzing with the vibrations of the strings. Annika managed to fit, at minimum, six hours of practice into her day and still have a life. She was on the debate team. She played field hockey. She said it was mostly to please her mother, who begged her to "expand her repertoire and live a little." The only thing Annika lived was cello.

Until I met Annika, until I came to St. Ives, I had no idea there were others like me. Addicts. People who sacrificed body and soul to be one with their art.

The picture of Annika playing, eyes closed, fingers flying across the strings, bowing fiercely, shifting effortlessly in rhythm with her head. It gave me chills. That first time we played a duet, the Sibelius *Canon*, I never felt so alive. The energy, the electricity. Literally, sparks between us. Last year we ripped the Ravel sonata. The frenetic, agitated ending. The last pizzicato chord punctuated the turbulent air.

We opened our eyes at the same time to the dull roar of applause, shouts of "brava." We looked at each other and knew. We knew. The fire burned through us. It was in her eyes, her face, her bow that trembled in her hand, same way mine did.

Was it my imagination? Did I wish it so hard I'd altered my own sense of reality?

How is that possible?

It'd been a year. A whole year trying to recapture that moment. Impossible to do without her. She lived in Maine. I lived in Utah. Half a country away. A lot could change in a year.

I'd changed. I'm not sure why or when, but suddenly I needed more than my music. It used to take everything I had to bring my music up from my very core; there was nothing left over. No time for games or groups or growing up; getting to know people. Surprise, Kat. There are other people in the world. It was like coming out of a seventeen-year coma. I know people at school thought I was a mole. Some dark, burrowing rodent that moved in the shadows. I didn't have friends. Not like Annika. She was the closest person to me, in heart and soul and mind.

She was going to cry when she saw me. We always cried at our reunions. We cried more when the three weeks ended and we had to return to our real lives. Last year I think I cried myself to sleep for a month. I missed her so much.

We couldn't afford long phone conversations.

We'd e-mail. She'd send me cards and notes throughout the year. Holiday greetings. "Thinking of You" cards.

She couldn't know how often I thought of her. And in what way. When did it start? I don't even know. Our last good-bye, clinging to each other, holding on until the very last second, until her father had to pry us apart.

Her mother said, "Kat, you know you're welcome to come to Maine and visit us anytime."

"Seriously." Annika held on to my hand. "Come for Thanksgiving. Or Christmas. Come spend your Christmas break with me."

I held her eyes.

She knew it was impossible. I didn't have money to go to Maine. I wouldn't let her pay either. Annika was here on scholarship too. Besides, there was Mom. She needed me. I was her only family, her baby.

Excuses, I know. I was afraid to go to Maine. Afraid for Annika to visit me. Terrified to alter the stasis of our relationship. Would we still be friends? Would it be the same?

Then there was Bryce. He lived in Boston. He and Annika saw each other all the time. They talked. They . . .

I shouldn't have come to camp. But I had no choice. I had to know. Would this be the beginning or the end? It'd be the longest three weeks of my life if Annika . . .

If she . . .

Rejected me.

Don't think about it, Kat. I squeezed my brain shut. You love St. Ives. You love it.

I did. I loved coming here, playing here. I'd won a full scholarship to continue attending through the end of high school. St. Ives was special, elite. It was a camp for musical prodigies.

We laughed at that too. I never believed I was a prodigy. I worked hard; we all did. We worked our butts off.

Even Bryce. He could work himself into oblivion.

The sign for Deer Creek Junction flew by so fast it only registered as a blip. I had to slam on the brakes and skid to a stop on a curve. Mom would have a heart attack if she saw that.

Sorry, Mom, I mentaled her. Distracted. I turned around.

Annika's last e-mail: "I know ur thinking about not coming. But u have to, Kat. U HAV 2. Do it 4 U."

Why didn't she say, "Do it 4 me?" Everything I did, I did for myself. The practicing, performing, planning for my future. If I had a future.

Annika had added, "Bryce calld last wk. He's coming 4 sur." A happy face.

The two of them had gone to the Met in New York. She'd flown to Boston on spring break.

My insides twanged a mass of snapped strings and frayed bows. The feelings, the longings. Not only for Annika, but for life on a human scale. A physical existence.

The duet, the Martinů, had sustained me all these months.

The look in her eyes. The chance, the hope that maybe there was more to us than music.

St. Ives. Ten more miles. Ten more minutes to Annika. Concentrate, Kat. Focus on the road. Don't think. Even if she doesn't return your feelings, it doesn't mean the world will end. A meteor won't crash to Earth and crush every living thing.

Yes, yes, it will. She has to love me back. If she doesn't, the fire inside me will die. The notes, the lyric — "I love you. I've always loved you" — had to be said, sung, shouted out loud.

I parked next to one of the St. Ives minivans. There were four now. They were used to haul groceries and supplies and instruments and musicians to concerts and competitions in surrounding valleys and mountain towns. The vans carted campers from the airport, or designated pickup points. I usually rode up in the van. Annika's parents drove her. All the way from Maine, they drove. Bryce came with them. They stayed in the same hotel. The same room?

Our final concert at the end of camp would draw a thousand people, easy. Parents and promoters and music school recruiters . . .

Music school.

This might be my final concert. I'd made my decision. If Annika rejected me, I was giving up the violin.

A chorus of giggles rose over the lake. Family groups paddleboating with their kids. There were more kids every year. More prodigies. As Annika and I got older, everyone else got younger. And better. More talented, it seemed. More determined. Or pushed. If I relented, if I took a break, forfeited my chair, there were scores of musical geniuses eager to take my place. Bryce would try to win back principal this year. All you had to do was watch him practice, see his soul leave his body as he became one with his cello, to know he had the fire.

Annika would watch him, mesmerized. She'd whispered once, "He's amazing. Isn't he?"

I grabbed my violin off the front seat and my duffel from the back. I got as far as the edge of the parking lot when I felt her. My eyes raised and saw her.

She was sitting at the top of the knoll, hugging her knees. She leapt to her feet, screaming, and tore down the hill. I set my duffel and violin case on the grass and started running too. We hit each other full speed, full tilt, and went flying. Grass and ground blurred my vision.

We rolled and rolled, wrapped in each other's arms. "Oh my God. Kat." Laughing and crying, Annika squeezed my face between her hands. "I was so afraid you weren't coming." Her face moved closer to mine, and I thought — prayed — she'd . . . please. At the last moment her lips veered away from mine and her cheek pressed against my face. Her arms smothered me in a suffocating hug.

I couldn't breathe. Not only because she'd rolled on top of me; she smelled like pancakes and pinecones and L'Air du Temps.

"Kat. Damn you!" Roughly, she pushed off. "Why didn't you write to me!" She pounded my shoulder into the ground.

"Ow. I did."

"Eight times," she said. "I wrote you eight hundred thousand times."

A million times, I didn't tell her. A million times I wrote to you. I couldn't press Send. I couldn't put the cards in the mail. The letters were too intimate. She had to hear this in person.

"Kat!" She clenched my face in a vise grip and pounded my head on the ground. "You cut your hair. I almost didn't know you."

Oh, Annika, I thought. Do you know me?

She looked at me, studied me, threw back her head and laughed. Then she hugged me again and rolled over, taking me with her. We tumbled off the grass and into the parking lot. Gravel crunched my spine.

She wouldn't let up. She clung, her body pressed to mine. She was shaking, heaving with laughter. Laughter? I tried to push away from her, but couldn't. She had me in a choke hold.

She squeezed my head so tight I couldn't think. "Annika?" My voice sounded high, out of range.

"Let me just make sure you're here," she said. She crushed me one last time in an embrace. Then flung herself away and scrabbled to sit, yanking me up beside her.

We both exhaled long breaths. She smiled. I smiled. She said, "I love it."

My whole body seized. "What?"

"Your hair."

"Oh." I deflated. "Yeah, well. It looks better without the grass and dirt." I bent forward and tousled my hair with my hands. Right after I made my decision to come, I'd had my hair chopped and streaked blue and maroon. I don't know why. It wasn't like me. What was like me?

She scooted back onto the lawn and tugged on my shirt. I scrabbled up next to her. Touching shoulders, we looked, then looked away.

She lifted hair out of her eyes with the back of her wrist.

"You got your hair cut too," I said.

"Oh yeah. Drastic." She feathered her bangs.

Her hair was beautiful, curly or straight. But I didn't care about her hair.

"Annika —"

"Where is —?" She leaned forward and glanced around the van. "Oh God." She held her heart. "For a minute I thought you didn't bring your violin."

I choked. Literally. Annika laughed. It made me laugh. We both knew how ridiculous that was. My violin was an appendage, like her cello. I almost asked where it was, but enough stalling.

Extending my legs, I began again, "Annika."

She took a deep breath and let it out. Slowly, deliberately, she twisted to face me. "Yes, Kat." She fluttered her eye-lashes.

Dammit, don't joke around, I thought.

I swallowed the lump in my throat. Chunks I'd been blow-ing for a week. "I have to tell you something."

Annika pressed two fingers to my lips. "Shut up. It's been a year."

Her fingers moved across my cheek and spread apart. Her other hand found my other cheek. With her thumbs under my chin, she drew me close. She kissed me.

Martinů played in my head. Finely tuned, fiercely pitched. We came apart, our lips making a soft suction sound, a con-ductor's baton. I locked on her eyes.

"What?" she said.

"Bryce."

She made a face. "What about him?"

"Are you . . . ? Does he . . . ?"

She hunched her shoulders and lifted her palms. "What?"

"You said you're glad he's coming."

She scoffed. "Well, yeah. He's my only competition. I plan to beat the crap out of him again." She cocked her head. "Why? What'd you think?"

I couldn't speak. My heart roared in my ears. I said the only thing I could. "I was scared. So scared you —" My throat constricted.

"Kat, I swear." Annika shook her head. Then pinched me on the arm.

Ow.

"All these years," she said. "All this time." Her eyes filmed. "You're tone-deaf, you know that? You never could pick up the beat." She exhaled disgust, or something, then caressed my cheek again. I transferred the weight of my head to her hand. The weight of it.

"You always come in late," Annika said. She pressed her forehead to mine. "Tune in, girl. I love you."